MIGHTY, MIGHTY RAIDERS

Ron Drost

MIGHTY, MIGHTY, RAIDERS
A Novel

Cover design by Ron Drost
Interior design by Ron Drost

Printed in the United States of America
Published by Static Signal Press
First Edition

ISBN: 979-8-234-01400-9

Dedicated to my sons
Eric & Ethan…

CONTENTS

WHERE KINDNESS TOOK ROOT

Galesburg, Pennsylvania is one of those towns you pass through on your way to somewhere else. There are no tourist attractions, only abandoned coal mines. There are no fancy restaurants, only hearty ethnic meals served each night in the homes of hard-working, lower-middle-class families, most of whom descend from Eastern European immigrants. There are no art or cultural centers, only sacred family traditions handed down from generation to generation during holiday gatherings. There are no entertainment venues, only a small movie theater tucked behind a shopping plaza with half its storefronts vacant. Yet what Galesburg lacks in civic amenities, it more than compensates for in the spirit of its people.

Cy Mozatta was of Italian descent and grew up in a part of town where most Italian immigrants who arrived in the late 1800s and early 1900s to work the coal mines had settled. It was a proud Italian neighborhood, made evident by the green, white, and red stripes painted on many of the telephone poles lining the streets — a gesture meant to honor the colors of the homeland.

In this neighborhood, everyone knew everyone else — sometimes a little too well — as much of the evening's entertainment revolved around discovering something new about a neighbor to gossip about at church on Sunday. Front doors were always left unlocked, not because there was little of value inside, but because of the deep sense of safety that came from living in a close-knit community. Children roamed the streets after school, playing tag and riding their bikes until their mothers called them in for dinner, one voice after another echoing down the block. The air was often filled with the subtle aromas of home cooking, and people could be seen sitting on their porches at day's end, sipping homemade wine and waving to passersby. Life here was simple but deeply fulfilling, centered around family and community.

Cy's father worked in the coal mines like most fathers in town, struggling to earn enough to pay the bills and hopefully have a little left over at week's end to spend on his family. A movie or a trip to a nearby ice cream shop served as the family's reward for a father's long, grueling week in the mines.

Cy's parents were the same age and met while still in high school. They married shortly after graduation when his father secured steady work in the #7 mine. It was another twelve years before Cy was born, after his parents had saved enough to feel secure bringing a child into their home. Cy's father died just six years later from leukemia. His battle with the disease was brief; eighteen years in the mines has a way of stripping a person's will to live.

What Cy remembered most from his short time with his father was the game of catch they played each Sunday afternoon with an old football. He remembered it as if it were yesterday — the smell of the worn leathery hide, scuffed from all the passes he had dropped; the sight of the football spiraling tightly across the deep blue sky, occasionally brushing past wispy clouds; the sound of birds squawking at him and his father for disturbing their lunch at the feeder his mother always kept full. It was in those moments that his love for the game first took root.

Cy had known from an early age that he had little chance of leaving the area. He struggled just to get by in school, and although he was a very good football player in high school, he was a lineman — an offensive guard, to be exact. No college ever recruited linemen from this region, especially not one who stood 5'9" and weighed barely 190 pounds. A Division II school might occasionally visit to scout a promising quarterback or running back from a nearby town, but never a lineman, and certainly never in Galesburg.

After high school, Cy took a job delivering processed anthracite coal from the local mines to the many residents who still used coal stoves to heat their homes. At the end of each day, just like his father before him, he returned home tired and dirty, covered in the fine black coal dust that clung to everything and was an unavoidable hazard of working with the "black diamonds," the lifeblood of the region and the reason his ancestral family had come here in the first place.

Cy met his wife Joanne at work; she was the daughter of the owner and worked in a small office near the front of the main building, where she handled customer invoices. Cy saw her only once each morning as he passed her office on the way to the garage at the rear of the building, but those brief moments became a cherished ritual. He would glance in and offer a friendly "Good morning," and she would respond with a warm, "Good morning, Cy, hope you have a special day," a simple exchange that somehow made him forget his troubles.

An unexpected late-winter storm finally gave Cy the chance to get to know Joanne better. The roads were so treacherous that even the largest delivery trucks couldn't operate, and the downtime allowed them to talk. In the days that followed, those conversations became a quiet ritual — first out of circumstance, then by choice. Cy found himself lingering a little longer near the front office each morning, offering an extra comment or small joke just to hear her laugh. Joanne, usually reserved and focused on her work, began stepping out during her breaks, pretending she needed fresh air when she was really hoping Cy might be near.

They discovered small but meaningful overlaps in their lives: both had grown up without much money, both carried a sense of responsibility heavier than their years, and both believed that kindness — simple, everyday kindness — was the only thing that made life bearable in a place like Galesburg. Cy admired the way Joanne treated everyone with the same kind respect, whether it was the company's wealthiest client or the janitor sweeping coal dust from the hallway. Joanne, in turn, admired Cy's steadiness, the way he listened without rushing to speak, the way he seemed to carry the burdens of others as naturally as breathing.

What Cy discovered behind that comforting voice was a kind and compassionate woman — someone who fed stray animals despite barely having enough money for herself, someone who gave up a chance to attend college and leave the depressed region so she could help run the family business, someone who always smiled and never complained about life's hardships. And Joanne discovered in Cy a man who never boasted, never pretended to be more than he was, and never hesitated to help anyone who needed it. Their connection grew quietly, without grand gestures or dramatic declarations — just two people finding warmth in each other during a season when everything else felt cold.

It was easy for Cy to fall in love. What surprised him was how naturally their lives began to intertwine after that winter. Cy and Joanne kept finding excuses to talk — short conversations at first, then longer ones that stretched past closing time. They shared stories about their childhoods, their families, their hopes for a future that neither of them had ever dared to imagine too boldly.

Cy admired the quiet strength beneath Joanne's gentle manner, and Joanne found comfort in Cy's steadiness, the way he listened as if every word she spoke mattered.

They started taking evening walks through town, always telling themselves it was just to get some fresh air after a long day. But those walks became the highlight of their routines. They learned each other's rhythms — how Cy paused before answering difficult questions, how Joanne tucked her hair behind her ear when she was nervous, how both of them laughed a little too loudly when the other made a joke. There was nothing dramatic about their courtship; it grew the way seasons change, slowly but unmistakably.

By the time summer arrived, everyone around them could see what they themselves had only recently begun to admit: they were inseparable. Cy would show up early just to carry boxes for Joanne before her shift, and Joanne would stay late to help him finish paperwork he insisted he didn't need help with. Their coworkers teased them gently, but neither minded. For the first time in their lives, they felt seen — truly seen — by someone who understood the weight they carried and didn't judge them for it.

When Cy finally asked Joanne to marry him, he did it in the simplest way he knew how. They were sitting on the back steps of her family's business at dusk, watching the last employees drift away. He told her he didn't have much to offer — no fancy ring, no big house, no promise of an easy life. What he did have, he said, was a heart that belonged entirely to her and a determination to build something better together than either of them had been given. Joanne didn't hesitate. She took his hands, smiled that quiet, steady smile he loved, and said yes.

Their wedding was small, held in the modest church both families had attended for generations. There were no elaborate decorations, no expensive dresses or catered meals — just a gathering of people who cared for them, who knew the hardships they had endured, and who believed they deserved a little happiness. Cy remembered standing at the front of the church, his palms sweating, his heart pounding, until Joanne walked in wearing a simple white dress her mother had sewn. In that moment, everything else faded. He knew he had made the best decision of his life.

After the ceremony, they shared a humble reception in the church basement — homemade dishes, mismatched chairs, laughter echoing off the walls. It wasn't grand, but it was warm, genuine, and filled with the kind of love that doesn't need embellishment. When they left that night, hand in hand, they stepped into a future that neither of them could fully picture yet, but both were determined to face it together.

A few years after they married, Cy and Joanne moved into Cy's childhood home to care for his ailing mother, who passed away during their first year there. Two years later, on a cold November morning, their son Tom was born. As Cy held his newborn for the first time, he remembered what it felt like to grow up without a father — to have no one to play catch with, to go fishing with, to learn from, to teach him the countless small things only a father can pass on. To have no hero. That day, Cy made a promise to himself that he would do everything in his power to give Tom the opportunities he never had, to give him a better life.

INSPIRATION

Tom had a fairly typical childhood — at least typical for Galesburg. He spent his days playing with friends on the discarded heaps of shale and coal left behind by decades of mining. While most people saw a landscape scarred and exhausted, littered with rusting machinery and riddled with dangerous sinkholes, Tom saw something wondrous. To him, it was a place filled with ancient fossils of ferns and long-extinct plants unearthed by mining operations, a place dotted with swimming holes formed by spring rains that filled abandoned dredged pits, a place full of old mineshafts perfect for exploring or hiding during late-summer games of hide-and-seek. Tom had always been able to see the best in everything and everyone.

Like most boys his age, Tom was also drawn to sports. Each weekend, he and neighborhood friends played sandlot football — though in Galesburg, the "sandlot" was actually a section of mining property where small pieces of coal, about the size of coarse sand, were discarded and leveled to create a parking area for mine employees. On weekends, that same space transformed into a battleground where last-second touchdowns won imaginary championships of the universe.

Tom learned football from his father, and he likely never realized how meaningful those moments were to Cy. For Cy, playing catch with Tom allowed him to step back into a place that existed long ago, when he and his own father performed the same ritual in their backyard. Although the memories had faded, the feeling remained — the feeling of having a hero right in front of you. It's something you rarely understand when you're young, and sometimes the realization comes too late to say thank you.

Tom was now ten years old and showing a genuine interest in football — more than the casual curiosity of a boy trying different sports. Cy could see raw talent in him and wondered whether this might be Tom's path to a better life, a way out of Galesburg. He knew every father must dream of such possibilities for his son, but he wanted to ensure Tom at least had the opportunity. So he talked to him about joining a youth football team where he could begin learning the fundamentals. Tom responded with enthusiasm, and Cy began searching for information on local leagues.

Cy assumed there must be a Pop Warner or similar program nearby where boys Tom's age could learn the game and, more importantly, the values of sportsmanship and teamwork. Because Cy's father died when he was six, he never played organized football until his sophomore year of high school, when he joined the team mostly to have something to do after school besides hanging out at the local pizza shop.

Cy began his search at town hall at the Parks and Recreation Department. One Friday during lunch, he drove to the most prominent building in town, constructed during the population boom when immigrants flooded the region and the town needed more space for its records. The building's façade was impressive and imposing, with two large stone columns flanking the main entrance. Inside, a grand marble staircase wound up to the second floor, where open corridors surrounded various offices, looming overhead as if demanding respect.

Turning his attention back to the task at hand, Cy searched several corridors until he found a sign pointing toward the town clerk responsible for the Parks and Recreation Department. To his disappointment, the clerk knew of no youth football league registered with the office. However, the clerk did mention that, to the best of his knowledge, the first opportunity for a boy to play football in Galesburg was in Junior High School. He followed this statement with a curt outburst: "No wonder our high school team never wins. These guys need more time to learn how to play the game."

As startled as Cy was by the comment, he couldn't deny its accuracy. During the three years he played high school football, the team won only four games — one of them by forfeit when most of the visiting team suffered an untimely bout of the flu. Although Cy hadn't followed his alma mater closely after graduation, he was well aware of the team's losing record year after year. It had become a sore spot for most of the town.

Other towns in the region fielded seasoned high school squads — or at least that's how it appeared to the people of Galesburg. Every Friday night in the chilly fall air, the Galesburg High School team took the field, and almost every Friday night they walked off wondering when they might taste victory again. Losing became easy, almost expected. Without even the occasional win to keep hope alive, motivation dwindled, making it even harder to break the cycle.

Despite the team's struggles, the people of Galesburg still filled the stands at Harmon Stadium for Friday night home games. While it was partly an excuse to get out of the house, it was also a chance to forget their daily troubles and dream that maybe — just maybe — this would be the night Galesburg triumphed. It was like playing the lottery: the odds were stacked against them, but if there was even a one-in-a-million chance of winning, people could convince themselves the impossible might be possible. And so the weekly ritual continued.

Most losses were accepted with resignation, but the one that stung the most — the one that could dampen the town's spirit for days — was the annual game against Haleyville, another mining town about ten miles east of Galesburg. No one could prove it, but enough corroborating stories circulated about the origins of the rivalry that most people accepted them as truth. Apparently, in the early 1900s, many coal mines had football teams unofficially sponsored by mine owners. Games were played on Saturday mornings and served as the primary civic event of the week. Clergy, teachers, shop owners, wives, and children all came out to watch grown men battle on dusty fields, competing mostly for bragging rights and the occasional tin trophy. Unknown to the spectators, mine owners often placed large wagers on the outcomes.

As the story went, in 1919 the Galesburg #5 mine team played the only mine team in Haleyville. Haleyville won by six points after a dramatic last-minute score. Days later, in a local bar, a Galesburg player — after one too many drinks — bragged that Galesburg would have won easily if not for his deliberate missed tackle that allowed the final touchdown. Further investigation revealed that the Haleyville mine boss had paid several Galesburg players to throw the game. From that moment on, a fierce rivalry took root, with Haleyville winning most of the recent matchups.

After leaving the clerk's office, Cy returned to work and eventually home. Though discouraged, he wasn't ready to give up on finding an opportunity for Tom to play organized football. Knowing Haleyville's high school program was strong, he became convinced there must be a "feeder" system there — some youth program that gave their boys a head start long before Junior High.

The very next day, Cy drove to Haleyville. With little effort, he coaxed information from a local gas station owner about the town's youth football league. Being a Saturday near the end of August, he was fortunate to learn that the teams were practicing at the local recreation fields not far from the station.

When Cy arrived, he could hardly believe what he saw: at least a dozen teams spread across as many fields, each engaged in its own practice routine. Every team had its own colors, vivid against the bright green grass. Each player wore a full uniform — shoulder pads, bright white pants occasionally stained green, and helmets that looked two sizes too big. Coaches wore matching shirts, displaying their pride. Across the way, cheerleading squads barked out cheers, motivating players even though it was only practice. Footballs sailed through the air as parents gathered on the sidelines to socialize, their younger children playing in the soft grass. It was a remarkable sight.

Cy immediately recognized that this was likely why Haleyville dominated Galesburg year after year. By the time these boys reached high school, they had accumulated years of experience that Galesburg players lacked.

Cy moved closer to one of the practice fields and waited for a pause in the conversation between two fathers standing along the sideline. When the moment came, he introduced himself and explained that he had a ten-year-old son eager to play football, and he was hoping to learn what options existed for joining a youth league.

One of the fathers replied, "Well, sir, you're talking to the right person. I happen to be on the league admissions committee." Then, almost immediately, he asked, "How long have you lived in Haleyville?"

Cy hesitated before answering. "Oh, I don't live here. I actually live in Galesburg."

"Well, unfortunately, this league is only open to town residents," the man said, his tone carrying a faint but unmistakable hint of condescension at the mention of Galesburg.

"I see," Cy responded politely. "Sorry to interrupt your conversation. Have a good day." He turned and walked away.

As he made his way back to his car, Cy felt a wave of helplessness wash over him. It seemed likely that Tom would have no opportunity to play competitive football until Junior High. He sat in the driver's seat for a moment, staring at the scene before him. The longer he watched, the more he noticed the subtle exchanges between fathers on the sidelines and their sons on the field — silent communications that spoke volumes. It was the kind of thing captured by the phrase "a picture is worth a thousand words," though in this case, it was more like "a gesture is worth a thousand words."

Cy watched one boy make a seemingly impossible catch, tumble to the ground, and immediately look toward his father for approval. The father responded with a thumbs-up and a small, proud nod. Cy could almost see the smile beneath the boy's facemask as he ran back to the huddle, eager for the next play. A pang of jealousy struck Cy, followed by a deep sadness. How incredible it would be, he thought, to stand on the sideline and watch Tom make a catch like that. The thought lingered as he started the car and drove away.

On the drive home, Cy couldn't stop thinking about how to make that vision a reality. He wondered whether other nearby towns might have youth programs willing to accept boys from outside their borders. But the next closest town was twenty miles farther than Haleyville. Even if they accepted out-of-town players, how would he get Tom to practice every night without jeopardizing his job or Tom's homework time? There had to be another way.

As he drove, faint ideas began to take shape — thoughts he tried to dismiss as unrealistic. Maybe he could start a youth football league in Galesburg. Each time the idea surfaced, he pushed it aside, but it kept returning, as if insisting on being heard.

The more he tried to ignore it, the more plausible it began to feel. Every time he imagined an obstacle, a possible solution seemed to appear. Slowly, excitement began to build inside him — the kind of excitement you feel the night before a long-awaited summer vacation, or when a friend tells you the girl you like has been asking about you, or for that matter, the excitement that must come from watching your son make that great catch.

The more Cy thought about it, the more details he worked out. He pulled into the parking lot of a small grocery store so he could write everything down before the ideas slipped away. He hurried inside, grabbed a small notebook and a pen, and fumbled for his wallet, dropping both items in his rush to reach the checkout. The cashier noticed his flustered state and asked, "Is everything all right, sir?"

Cy smiled and said, "Couldn't be better!" He sat in that parking lot for almost an hour, his pen seemingly never lifting from the paper.

EVOLUTION OF AN IDEA

Cy's mind raced as he filled page after page with ideas, sketching out everything from how teams might be organized to where practices could be held. He thought about equipment, coaches, volunteers, and how to convince the town that such a league was not only possible but necessary. The more he wrote, the more the plan seemed to take on a life of its own, as if it had been waiting inside him for years, needing only the right moment to emerge.

He imagined Tom wearing a uniform for the first time, running onto a field with teammates, learning plays, building confidence, and discovering the joy of competition. He pictured the pride he would feel standing on the sideline, watching his son grow not just as an athlete but as a young man. The thought filled him with a sense of purpose he hadn't felt in years.

Cy knew the road ahead would be difficult. He would need support from the town, cooperation from schools, and help from parents who were already stretched thin. He would need to navigate bureaucracy, raise money, and convince people that a youth football league could make a difference in a place where hope often felt in short supply. But as he sat in his car with the notebook open on his lap, he felt something he hadn't felt in a long time — optimism.

He closed the notebook and took a deep breath, letting the weight of the moment settle in. For the first time since he had watched the boys practicing in Haleyville, he felt a sense of control over Tom's future. Maybe he couldn't change the past, and maybe he couldn't erase the hardships that had shaped his own life, but he could try to build something better for his son. Something lasting. Something meaningful.

Cy started the car and pulled out of the parking lot, the notebook resting on the passenger seat like a promise. He didn't know exactly how he would make the league a reality, but he knew he had to try. For Tom. For the town. For every boy who deserved a chance to dream bigger than the coal-scarred hills surrounding Galesburg.

As he drove home, the sun dipped low on the horizon, casting long shadows across the road. Cy felt a renewed sense of determination rising within him. He had an idea, a plan, and a reason to fight for it. And sometimes, he thought, that was enough to change everything.

Cy drove the rest of the way home with a sense of purpose that felt almost foreign to him. For years, life had been something that happened to him — work, bills, routine, responsibility — but now he felt as though he was steering toward something meaningful. The idea of a youth football league in Galesburg was no longer just a passing thought; it was becoming a mission. He knew it would take time, effort, and persistence, but he also knew that anything worthwhile usually did.

When he arrived home, Tom ran out to greet him, full of energy and eager to share the details of his day. Cy watched his son's excitement and felt a renewed determination. This was who he was doing it for. This was the reason he had spent nearly an hour in a grocery store parking lot scribbling ideas into a notebook. He wanted Tom to have opportunities he never had, to feel the thrill of competition, to learn discipline and teamwork, and to discover the confidence that came from mastering something difficult.

That evening, after dinner, Cy sat at the kitchen table with his notebook open, reviewing the ideas he had written earlier.

Joanne walked in and noticed the intensity on his face. "What's all that?" she asked, setting down a cup of tea beside him.

Cy hesitated for a moment, unsure of how to explain the sudden burst of inspiration. "I think… I think I want to start a youth football league here in Galesburg," he finally said.

Joanne raised her eyebrows, surprised but not dismissive. "A football league? Here?"

"Yeah," Cy replied, flipping through the pages. "Tom wants to play, and there's nothing for kids his age. Haleyville has a whole system, and that's why their high school team is so good. Our boys don't get a chance to play until Junior High. It's not fair to them."

Joanne pulled out a chair and sat beside him. "It sounds like a big project."

"I know," Cy said, "but I think it's possible. And I think it could help a lot of kids, not just Tom."

She studied him for a moment, then smiled softly. "If anyone can do it, you can."

Her confidence in him was like fuel. Cy felt a surge of motivation, stronger than anything he had felt in years. He spent the rest of the evening outlining the first steps he would need to take — talking to town officials, finding fields, gathering volunteers, and figuring out how to pay for equipment. It was overwhelming, but it was also exhilarating.

Later that night, after Tom had gone to bed, Cy stepped outside onto the porch. The air was cool, and the sky was clear, dotted with stars. He leaned against the railing and let the quiet settle around him. For the first time in a long while, he felt hopeful. He didn't know exactly how everything would unfold, but he knew he had taken the first step. And sometimes, he thought, that was all it took to change the course of a life.

The next morning, Cy woke with a renewed sense of determination. The ideas he had written the night before still felt solid, and the excitement he had felt in the grocery store parking lot had not faded. He knew the first step would be to speak with town officials, but he also knew he needed to approach them with a clear plan. People in Galesburg were cautious about change, especially when it involved money or resources, and he wanted to be prepared for every question they might ask.

He spent part of the morning refining his notes, organizing them into sections:
- Purpose
- Benefits
- Logistics
- Costs
- Community involvement

The more he worked, the more confident he became. He imagined presenting the idea to the town council, explaining how a youth football league could help build pride, strengthen the high school program, and give children something positive to focus on. He imagined parents volunteering, local businesses sponsoring teams, and the community rallying behind something new and hopeful.

Later that week, Cy drove to town hall. The building looked just as imposing as it had during his previous visit, but this time he felt different. Instead of feeling small beneath its towering columns and marble staircase, he felt purposeful. He walked through the front doors, notebook in hand, and made his way to the office of the town clerk.

The clerk looked up as Cy approached. "Back again?" he asked, recognizing him from the week before.

"Yes," Cy said, offering a polite smile. "I'm working on something I think could help the kids in this town. I was hoping to speak with someone about starting a youth football league."

The clerk raised an eyebrow, clearly surprised. "A football league? Here?"

"That's right," Cy replied. "I've been thinking about it a lot. Our boys don't get to play until Junior High, and by then they're already behind. I think we can change that."

The clerk leaned back in his chair, considering the idea. "Well, you'll need to talk to the Parks and Recreation Committee. They handle anything involving fields or youth programs. They meet once a month."

"When's the next meeting?" Cy asked.

"Next Thursday evening," the clerk said. "Seven o'clock. You can sign up to speak."

Cy nodded, feeling a surge of anticipation. "Thank you. I'll be there."

As he left the building, he felt a mixture of nerves and excitement. He knew the meeting would be his first real test. He would need to convince a room full of people that his idea was worth supporting, that it could make a difference in a town that had grown accustomed to disappointment. But he also knew he had to try. For

Tom. For the community. For every kid who deserved a chance to feel proud of something.

That evening, Cy shared the news with Joanne. She listened intently, her expression warm and encouraging. "I think it's wonderful," she said. "And I think they'll listen to you."

"I hope so," Cy replied. "I really do."

He spent the rest of the night preparing for the meeting, rehearsing what he would say, imagining the questions he might be asked, and refining his notes until they felt just right. He knew he couldn't control how the committee would respond, but he could control how prepared he was. And he intended to be ready.

The days leading up to the meeting passed slowly, each one filled with a mix of anticipation and nervous energy. Cy continued refining his notes, rehearsing his presentation, and imagining how the committee might respond. He knew he needed to be clear, confident, and persuasive. He also knew that some people in town would resist the idea simply because it was new. Change didn't come easily to Galesburg, especially when it required effort or funding. But Cy believed in the idea, and that belief kept him focused.

On the evening of the meeting, Cy arrived at town hall early. The building once again looked imposing in the fading light, its stone columns casting long shadows across the steps. He took a deep breath before walking inside, clutching his notebook like a lifeline. The corridors were quiet, and the sound of his footsteps echoed off the marble floors as he made his way to the meeting room.

Inside, several committee members were already seated at a long table, shuffling papers and preparing for the evening's agenda. A few townspeople sat in folding chairs arranged in rows facing the front. Cy signed his name on the list of speakers and took a seat near the back, waiting for the meeting to begin. His heart pounded, but he reminded himself why he was there. He pictured Tom's face, full of excitement whenever they played catch, and the image steadied him.

The meeting began with routine business — budget updates, maintenance reports, and discussions about upcoming community events. Cy listened patiently, though his mind kept drifting to the moment when his name would be called. Finally, after nearly an hour, the chairman looked down at the list of speakers.

"Next, we have… Cy Mozatta," he announced.

Cy stood, smoothed the front of his shirt, and walked to the podium. He opened his notebook, took a breath, and began. "Thank you for giving me the opportunity to speak tonight. My name is Cy Mozatta, and I'm here because I believe our town's children deserve more opportunities — specifically, the chance to play organized football before they reach Junior High."

He explained how Galesburg's boys were at a disadvantage compared to those in neighboring towns, how they lacked early training, and how that affected the high school team's performance. He described the youth league he had seen in Haleyville — the uniforms, the coaches, the excitement — and how it had inspired him to imagine something similar for Galesburg. He outlined the benefits:

- Physical fitness
- Teamwork
- Discipline
- Community pride
- A stronger high school program in the long run

As he spoke, he noticed several committee members leaning forward, listening intently. Others remained expressionless, their faces unreadable. Cy continued, detailing possible practice locations, equipment needs, volunteer roles, and potential fundraising ideas. He emphasized that he wasn't asking the town to shoulder the entire burden; he was willing to help organize, recruit, and coordinate. He just needed their support to get started.

When he finished, the room was quiet for a moment. Then the chairman cleared his throat. "Thank you, Mr. Mozatta. That was… thorough." He glanced at the other committee members. "We'll open the floor for questions."

One member asked about liability. Another asked about costs. A third questioned whether enough children would participate to justify the effort. Cy answered each question as best he could, drawing on the notes he had prepared. He didn't have every answer, but he had enough to show he had thought things through.

After several minutes, the chairman nodded. "Thank you, Mr. Mozatta. We appreciate your initiative.

The committee will discuss this further and let you know our decision."

Cy thanked them and returned to his seat, his heart still racing. He didn't know whether he had convinced them, but he felt proud of himself for trying. As the meeting continued, he slipped out quietly, stepping into the cool night air. He looked up at the sky, feeling a mixture of hope and uncertainty. Whatever happened next, he knew he had taken an important step — not just for Tom, but for the entire town.

The week after the meeting felt unusually long. Cy found himself replaying the presentation in his mind, wondering whether he had said enough, whether he had sounded confident, whether the committee members had truly understood what the league could mean for the town. He tried not to dwell on it, but the uncertainty lingered. Still, he reminded himself that he had taken the first step, and sometimes that was the hardest part.

A few days later, while Cy was at work unloading coal from his truck, he heard someone calling his name. He turned to see one of the town council members approaching. The man waved as he drew closer. "Cy, got a minute?"

Cy wiped his hands on his pants and nodded. "Sure. Everything all right?"

The councilman smiled. "I just wanted to tell you that your presentation last week made an impression. The committee's still discussing it, but I think you've got some support. People can see how much you care."

Cy felt a flicker of hope. "I appreciate you saying that. I really believe this could help the kids."

"I know you do," the man replied. "And that matters. Sometimes passion is what gets things moving in this town." He gave Cy a reassuring nod before heading off.

The brief conversation lifted Cy's spirits. It wasn't a guarantee, but it was something — a sign that his idea was being taken seriously. That evening, he shared the news with Joanne, who smiled and squeezed his hand. "See? They're listening."

"I hope so," Cy said. "I really want this to work."

As the days passed, Cy continued thinking about the league, refining his ideas, and imagining how everything might come together. He pictured kids running drills on a field, parents cheering from the sidelines, and coaches teaching not just football skills but lessons about teamwork, discipline, and perseverance. He imagined the pride the town might feel watching its youth succeed, the way it could bring people together, the way it could give children something to look forward to.

One afternoon, while Cy was delivering coal to a customer, he found himself talking about the idea with the homeowner, an older man who had lived in Galesburg his entire life. The man listened thoughtfully before saying, "You know, this town could use something like that. Kids need something to keep them busy, something to be proud of. I hope they give you a chance."

Cy nodded, grateful for the encouragement. "I hope so too."

Word of Cy's idea began to spread slowly through the community. Some people were skeptical, unsure whether the town had the resources or the interest to support a youth football league. Others were enthusiastic, excited by the possibility of something new and positive for their children. Cy heard bits and pieces of conversations at the grocery store, at the gas station, and even at work. People were talking, and that alone felt like progress.

Still, Cy knew that talk wasn't enough. He needed action. He needed the committee's approval. And until he heard their decision, all he could do was wait — and hope.

The following Thursday arrived with a mixture of anticipation and unease. Cy had spent the entire week thinking about the committee's decision, replaying the meeting in his mind, and imagining every possible outcome. He tried to stay busy at work, but his thoughts kept drifting back to the league — how it might change Tom's life, how it might change the town, how it might give the children of Galesburg something to believe in. He reminded himself that whatever happened, he had done everything he could.

That evening, just as Cy and Joanne were finishing dinner, the phone rang. Cy wiped his hands on a towel and answered. On the other end was the chairman of the Parks and Recreation Committee. "Mr. Mozatta," the chairman began, "I wanted to let you know that the committee met again today to discuss your proposal."

Cy felt his heart begin to pound. "Yes, sir."

"We've decided," the chairman continued, "that your idea has merit. We believe a youth football league could benefit the town. It won't be easy, and there are still many details to work out, but we're willing to support the effort if you're willing to take the lead."

For a moment, Cy couldn't speak. Relief, excitement, and disbelief washed over him all at once. "Yes," he finally managed. "Yes, of course. I'm willing to do whatever it takes."

"Good," the chairman said. "Start thinking about volunteers, equipment, and potential practice locations. We'll help where we can."

"Thank you," Cy said, his voice thick with emotion. "Thank you so much."

After he hung up, he stood in the kitchen for a moment, letting the news sink in. Joanne watched him closely. "Well?" she asked.

"They said yes," Cy replied, a smile spreading across his face. "They're going to support the league."

Joanne let out a joyful laugh and threw her arms around him. "I knew they would. I'm so proud of you."

Cy felt a weight lift from his shoulders. For the first time, the dream felt real. There was still a long road ahead — planning, organizing, fundraising — but the door had been opened. The possibility had become a path.

LAYING THE GROUND WORK

Cy and Joanne sat together in the quiet of the kitchen, the weight of the moment settling over Joanne as she grasped the sheer scale of what lay ahead. The excitement of the idea remained, but now it was threaded with the sobering understanding that turning this dream into reality would demand far more time, money, and sacrifice than either of them had first imagined.

Joanne, hesitant to dampen Cy's spirits, reluctantly offered, "It's just that it's such a large undertaking. Where will you get the time, where will we get the money?"

Anticipating this, Cy felt his momentum return as he began outlining the solutions he had already been turning over in his mind. "First of all, we'll start small, and we have almost a year to get things ready for our first season," he said, reaching out to take her hand. "As for the money, I know at least two dozen business owners who'd be more than happy to diversify their advertising and sponsor a team. In fact, I plan to name the teams after the businesses that sponsor them." He held her gaze, wanting her to see how deeply he believed in this. "I've come up with a half-dozen ideas to raise money for the league. Heck, we can have the kids sell raffle tickets and learn about economics at the same time," he added with a wink.

"I also plan to ask Paul Vittel down at the Public Works Department if we can use the fields behind the town garage for practices and games. I'm sure he won't mind if I promise we'll keep them up in return," Cy continued, barely pausing for breath as idea after idea spilled out. "I'm sure I can get some of my old high school teammates to coach, and the rest we'll fill in with parents. And you know Bob — the big guy who always sits in the first pew at church? Well, he owns Bob's Sporting Goods on Spruce Street, and he owes me a few favors from back in high school. I'm sure he'll give us equipment and uniforms at wholesale."

Joanne listened, recognizing that Cy's years in Galesburg — delivering coal, helping neighbors, building relationships — had left him unusually well connected.

Bankers, business owners, town officials…the very people he would need to make this dream real.

"Wow," she said, still skeptical but undeniably impressed. "You certainly seem to have thought things through. And all this from that first epiphany while sitting in a grocery store parking lot?"

But as Cy continued, diving deeper into the details in an effort to erase the last traces of doubt in her mind, Joanne felt herself swept up in his enthusiasm. She could see how much this meant to him. And knowing how much it would mean to Tom, she wrapped her arms around Cy and said, "Let's go for it."

To Cy, that hug felt like it lasted a lifetime.

The next day, he began the long journey toward making his dream a reality. The first and most critical task, he decided, was securing a place for the teams to practice and play.

Cy had first met Paul Vittel during a fierce Nor'easter five years earlier, when Cy volunteered to drive a snowplow. The storm had lasted more than two days, and the department was short on drivers. Since Cy had experience driving a coal truck — similar in size to the town's plows — he stepped in, grateful for the extra pay so close to Christmas.

Over time, Cy became a regular substitute driver, filling in when needed. Between shifts, he and Paul bonded over quick poker games in the supervisor's office. Their friendship had grown naturally, and Cy knew he could count on Paul now.

After a quick phone call and a short drive, Cy met Paul at a small tavern near Paul's house. The place was cramped, converted from a private residence after Prohibition, and packed with people drinking beer and watching a ball game on the TV above the bar.

Cy and Paul managed to grab two seats after a pair of men left to join friends. Cy ordered two drafts, paying quickly with a crisp dollar bill.

"Thanks, I'll get the next round," Paul said.

"You may change your mind after you hear what I'm about to ask," Cy joked.

He took a long sip of beer, then launched into the same pitch he had given Joanne. The tavern was loud, forcing Paul to lean in, arm around Cy's shoulder, as Cy raised his voice to be heard.

Just as Cy finished explaining the youth football league, a rough voice cut through the noise.

"Youth football league? Hell, it's about time this town had something for these kids to do. Maybe now they'll stop vandalizing my equipment."

Cy and Paul turned to see a burly man in a plaid shirt, open over a stained tee, beer in one hand and a half-smoked cigarette in the other.

"Joe Muscovitz, owner of All State Construction," he said. "Couldn't help overhearing. You seriously going to do this? Put together a football league for these kids?"

Annoyed by the interruption, Cy replied, "That's the plan. Why — want to sponsor a team?"

"Well, if there's even a slim chance it keeps the neighborhood delinquents away from my equipment, then yes, I will," Joe said.

"Are you serious?" Cy asked.

"About as serious as I am about finishing this beer and smoke."

"Let's move to the back where it's quieter," Cy said, raising his voice over the sudden roar of the crowd reacting to a big play on the TV.

Paul went ahead to find a table. Cy introduced himself to Joe, who crushed his cigarette under his boot before shaking Cy's hand. The three men settled into a corner table in the quieter back room.

After Cy recapped the parts Joe had missed, both Paul and Joe bought in immediately. Whether it was love of football, town pride, or the hope of finally beating Haleyville High School again, Cy didn't know. But he now had two more believers — and potentially his first team sponsor.

Paul agreed to bring the idea of using the Public Works fields to the town council. He was confident they'd approve it, especially since they'd been pressuring him to clean up the overgrown, rodent-ridden area anyway. A deal where the youth league maintained the fields in exchange for using them seemed like a win-win.

The men toasted their ideas, and when Cy finally noticed the clock, nearly three hours had passed. He downed the rest of his beer.

"Gotta get home or the wife's going to give me hell. I promised her I'd fix the washer today." Cy said this only to save face with the guys; he knew with all the time he was spending plotting out the details of his plan he had been neglecting the chore for quite some time and deserved whatever verbal punishment Joanne was planning on dishing out.

As they stood to leave, Cy placed a hand on Joe's shoulder. "So, what nickname are you giving your team?"

Joe paused, then said, "The All State Construction Oilers." He chose the name after his favorite professional franchise, the Houston Oilers — a team he had followed passionately since childhood. His loyalty ran deeper than simple fandom; his uncle had served as a special teams coach for the Oilers for two years, a connection that explained why Joe defied local tradition by supporting them instead of either of the two Pennsylvania NFL teams.

Cy and Paul exchanged a knowing look. The league was going to happen.

On the way home, Cy knew he still had much to do and many obstacles to overcome. But in his mind the biggest one — finding a home for his league — was well on its way to being resolved, and he had the added bonus of possibly securing his first team "owner" as well. He took a moment to reflect on everything that had happened over the past few hours and couldn't help but wonder what the future might hold. Before reaching home, Cy told himself he was done obsessing over his plan for the day; after all, he'd soon need to focus on fixing the washer.

Cy did fix the washer that evening, but no matter how much he tried to focus on other things, he couldn't stop thinking about all the details needed for the league to succeed. As he did, Cy began to wonder if his attention to the task was driven only by its newness and novelty. He questioned whether his drive would sustain itself for the many months ahead. He thought about the possibility of investing so much time and money into developing his idea only to have something unexpected happen that ended it all. What if kids didn't want to play? What if there just weren't enough kids in town to fill the league? Cy started to feel overwhelmed and knew he had to do something to put his mind at ease.

Cy found Joanne upstairs in Tom's room folding clothes. One look at his face told her something was wrong. Assuming it had to do with the league, Joanne set the clothes aside, sat on the bed, and said lightheartedly, "So, let me guess — you're obsessing about all the stuff you have ahead of you, and now you're overwhelmed and thinking about giving it all up."

Amazed by his wife's seemingly clairvoyant statement, Cy nodded, his lips tucked away much like a dog tucks its tail between its legs when defeated.

"You have to slow down or you'll burn yourself out," Joanne declared. Her tone shifted. "I don't want you to do anything more on this for at least a week," she said firmly. "I mean nothing!"

Cy considered his reply carefully. "You're right," he said. "I have a busy week at work anyway; we're finishing up the job at the Alter Street Café." He was referring to a remodeling job he was doing for a local contractor. Cy also worked part-time as a builder when coal deliveries were sparse. It allowed him to guarantee steady income so Joanne didn't have to work and could stay home with Tom. Both felt it was important to have a parent around full-time to raise their son.

"I'll make you a deal," Cy said. "I'll do my best to only work on this during weekends, which should keep it fresh for me, and that way it won't interfere with my job either. But there may be some things I have to take care of during the week. I'll just keep those to a minimum." He extended his hand to Joanne.

Joanne grasped his hand and replied with a touch of sarcasm, "It's a deal — as long as you keep up with the stuff around the house too, like fixing appliances when they break. Oh, and you also have to make time to spend with Tom — you know, your son…the reason you're doing all this!" She wanted to remind Cy not to lose sight of what truly mattered.

"Deal," Cy said.

For the most part, Cy managed to keep his mind off the league for a few days — until he received a phone call one evening from Paul.

"Guess who is now the official Galesburg Youth Football League President and overseer of its brand-new practice facility?" shouted Paul as Cy picked up the receiver.

"You're kidding — they actually went for it!" Cy responded.

"Yep, they gave me the answer today. But you have to promise you'll follow through and take full responsibility for keeping the fields in good shape. Oh, and the town council wants all the kids to sign a waiver saying they won't hold the town liable if they get hurt while playing there," Paul stipulated. "Other than that, they're yours for the taking."

"Sure, yeah, no problem — whatever it takes," Cy said, barely able to contain his excitement. "Thanks, buddy, I owe you one."

"Forget it," Paul replied. "You're doing me a favor, remember?"

"I won't let you down," Cy said. "Let me get going — I have to call Joe and give him the good news. I sure hope he was serious about sponsoring a team. I get the feeling I'm going to be needing his money pretty damn soon."

Cy hung up and immediately dialed Joe, figuring the big news justified calling even though it wasn't the weekend.

After a few rings, a woman answered.

"Can I speak to Joe, please?" Cy asked politely.

"Whom should I say is calling?" she replied.

"Tell him it's Cy Mozatta, President of the Galesburg Youth… no, wait — President of the Greater Galesburg Athletic Club," Cy announced proudly, feeling the revised title sounded more official.

"…Just a minute," the voice said after a slight hesitation, as if processing the importance of the title.

During the silence while she went to get Joe, Cy reflected on how pleased he was with the new name he'd chosen for the league. G… G… A… C…, he thought. Perfect!

"Hey Cy!" Joe's voice came through the phone. "My wife warned me you might be someone looking for a donation. I had to laugh inside because she didn't know just how right she was!" Joe joked.

"That's funny," Cy replied. "Now that you mention it, my wife did something similar a few days ago — actually predicted what I was thinking. Must be that woman's intuition thing I keep hearing about." The two men laughed.

"Anyway," Cy continued, "Paul called earlier and told me we have the fields! I just wanted to give you the good news and get a firm commitment that you still want to sponsor one of the teams."

"More committed than ever," Joe said confidently. "I've actually been thinking about where to put the trophy after my team wins the league championship."

"You seem to have more trust in this idea than I do," Cy cautioned. "This is just the beginning — it's not a done deal yet. But now that I have the fields and your word on sponsoring a team, I can start investing more time and money into this thing. I'll call you back in a few weeks after I see how many other teams and sponsors I can scrape up. Then we can talk about the sponsorship fee."

"Fair enough," Joe said. "And let me know if there's anything else I can do to help."

"Well, I can certainly use some help recruiting those team sponsors," Cy admitted. "You're well connected in the Chamber of Commerce."

"No problem — I'll bring it up at the next meeting. Most of those guys own their businesses, and a lot of them have young sons too. Don't worry — we'll fill up this league in no time!" Joe exclaimed.

"Thanks again — this is the boost I needed to get this project off the ground," Cy said. "Talk to you soon." He hung up.

All Cy could think about was how easy things had been so far. The thought made him nervous — he knew tough times were bound to find him eventually. He pushed the worry aside and went to share the good news with Joanne.

A few days later, Cy decided it was time to visit an old high school football teammate, hoping to persuade him to take on a coaching role in the new league. Stan Bosch had played beside Cy on the offensive line and served as the team's kicker during their junior and senior years. The two had become close friends, and it was Cy who had given him the nickname "Stosh," a name Stan had embraced ever since. Stosh now worked as a mechanic at a local garage, and he and Cy stayed in touch regularly, as Cy brought all his vehicles there for service.

As Cy pulled into the service station parking lot, he spotted Stosh installing a rear tire on a delivery van perched high on a pneumatic lift. Cy eased his car into the adjacent oil change bay and gave a quick honk — just enough to get Stosh's attention without startling him as he lowered the heavy tire. Stosh turned, recognized him instantly, and grinned.

"A little soon for your next oil change, isn't it? Did ya take a trip or something lately?" he called out. Stosh's full-body coveralls were stained with years of oil and grease, and his hands and face bore the marks of a long day's work.

"No… no trip," Cy replied. "Here to talk to you about something, so I figured I'd just get ahead on my next oil change."

"Must be something really important then. The Cy I know doesn't waste money like that unless he has to," Stosh said, wiping his hands with a rag until they were clean enough for a handshake. "Let me get this tire balanced. We'll talk while I work — I just came off my break."

"Not a problem," Cy said. "I'll grab a cup of coffee. Yell when you're ready."

A few minutes later, Stosh waved him over. Once Cy's car was lifted and Stosh was beneath it, Cy launched into the story — how the idea had started, how it had grown, and how the town council had given its support. He focused on the essentials, knowing Stosh didn't have time for every detail.

"You're actually serious about doing this?" Stosh asked, his voice echoing slightly under the lift. "And Joanne is going to let you do this?" His expression carried a mix of doubt and amusement.

"Yes and yes," Cy answered. "Though I did have to make a few promises."

"Now that sounds like the Joanne I know," Stosh chuckled. "If you pull this off, it'll be a great thing for the town and the kids. But I know you didn't drive all the way here and get an oil change a thousand miles early just to tell me that."

"Well, no," Cy admitted. "I was hoping I could talk you into being one of the coaches. You love football, and being unattached... well, it seemed like a good fit."

Stosh paused, considering. "You've got my interest. I've never coached before, though. How old are these kids supposed to be?"

Cy hesitated. "Well... I haven't nailed that down yet. I figure it doesn't make sense to start them before eight. If I get enough kids and coaches, I'd like an introductory level — maybe eight to twelve — and then an advanced team that plays other towns." He shrugged. "Somewhere between eight and fifteen maybe? I'll sort out the details. So... what do you say?"

"Sure, what the hell. Count me in," Stosh said. "It'll give me a reason to get out of the apartment. Maybe I'll even meet one of those single soccer-type moms. I hear they're more desperate than the others — good news for this ugly mug." He laughed, brushing a hand over his long hair and beard, grown to hide the acne scars of his youth.

They talked through a few more details as Stosh finished the oil change. Before Cy left, Stosh added one condition: he wanted an assistant coach. Cy agreed immediately — he could have as many as he needed.

On the drive home, Cy replayed the conversation. The age groups, the structure, the levels of play — it all began to take shape. He liked the idea of an introductory level focused on fundamentals and sportsmanship. He remembered the chaos of high school games — the shouting parents, the fights in the stands, the pressure that crushed more than it inspired. He didn't want that for the youngest boys.

Cy also accepted that in order for kids to ultimately prepare themselves for the high school level, they needed to experience some sort of competitive play. He knew competition bred better performance and inspired a drive to improve, to practice harder, to take pride in one's accomplishments.

After some thought, Cy finalized that his league should have multiple levels of play. The lowest would be an introductory level, which he decided to call Pee-Wee, following the conventional Pop Warner name. This bottom level would be where any boy, regardless of skill, could learn the game's fundamentals. The next level he decided to call the Pony level, a name that suggested developing strength and skills beyond the basics — like a young horse somewhere between a foal and a stallion. The highest level he chose to call the Midget level, again following Pop Warner convention. He figured that at the Pony and Midget levels, he could either have a self-contained program with multiple teams or, even better, one Pony team and one Midget team that could play in an inter-city league. In that scenario, the Pony and Midget rosters would be chosen from the cream of the crop rising out of the Pee-Wee ranks.

He filed these options away in his mind to be resolved later and continued his drive home, satisfied by a few more key accomplishments.

The following Saturday, Cy drove to Bob's Sporting Goods to visit Bob Gallagher, another old high school acquaintance. Bob hadn't played football; instead, he had spent most of high school trying to avoid the cruelty of classmates who mocked him for his weight. Cy remembered the day their paths crossed.

One morning before school, Cy had seen several football players pushing a heavyset boy to the ground, scattering his books. Each time the boy tried to stand, someone shoved him back down, taunting him with, "Pigs walk on all fours where I come from." Cy had stormed across the street, furious.

"Too bad you guys don't apply this same intensity on the field!" he shouted.

"Stay out of this, Cy," Todd, the quarterback, warned.

"The hell I will," Cy shot back, pushing Todd away from the boy. Todd knew this wasn't the time or place to take on Cy and instead muttered, "I'll see YOU on the practice field."

"You can count on it," Cy replied.

After a tense stare-down, Todd walked away with the others. Cy reached out a hand to the boy.

"What's your name?" he asked.

"Bob," the boy said quietly.

"Don't worry about those guys, Bob. They need to pick on others because they don't like who they are inside. I'll make sure it doesn't happen again." Cy picked up Bob's notebook and handed it to him.

Just as Cy had promised, no one on the football team ever picked on Bob again. In fact, Cy became something of a bodyguard for him, making it clear that anyone who wanted to mess with Bob would have to go through him first.

Bob never forgot what Cy had done. He would later say that Cy was the reason he made it through high school at all. Bob eventually went on to community college, earned an associate degree in business management, and opened his sporting goods store a few years after graduation.

Now, years later, when Cy explained the league and its needs, Bob didn't hesitate. He promised to call suppliers, track down used equipment, and provide anything new at wholesale.

Funny how life comes full circle, Cy thought as he left the store.

With everything he had accomplished recently, Cy finally felt ready to tell Tom — amazed he had managed to keep it all a secret from him. When he arrived home, he found Tom struggling with his bicycle chain. Cy offered a deal: he'd fix the chain if Tom played catch with him afterward. Tom agreed instantly.

Soon the football was arcing through the air between them. After a few throws, Cy said, "Remember when we talked about you maybe joining a youth football league?"

Tom nodded. "Yeah. Last time we played catch."

"That's right," Cy said. "Well, I did some checking around and found there really aren't any options today." He saw disappointment flicker across Tom's face, so he quickly added, "But you know… tomorrow is another day."

Tom frowned. "What's that supposed to mean?"

Cy motioned him over and guided him to the porch steps, the wood still warm from the late-day sun. Tom sat beside him, legs swinging, waiting with that wide-open trust only a kid gives so freely. Cy took a breath, steadying himself. He didn't want to oversell it or drown the moment in details. He just wanted his son to feel the heartbeat of what was coming.

"I've been working on something," he began, his voice low and even. "Not just for me. For you. For a lot of kids in this town."

Tom's eyes lifted, curious.

"I'm building a league," Cy said. "A real one. I've got friends helping, people I trust. And if everything keeps moving the way it is… by next year, it should be ready."

He didn't mention the late nights, the phone calls, the favors he'd pulled, or the doubts he'd swallowed. None of that mattered right now. What mattered was the spark he saw ignite in Tom's face — that mix of surprise, pride, and something like relief, as if he'd been hoping for this without daring to say it out loud.

That was all Tom needed. He launched forward and wrapped his arms around his father's waist, squeezing with all the strength his small frame could muster. Cy closed his eyes and let the moment wash over him. The porch, the quiet yard, the smell of cut grass — it all faded behind the simple truth of his son's arms around him.

This, he thought, *is what it's all about. This is why you push. This is why you keep going.*

Tom squeezed harder, his voice muffled against Cy's shirt. "Are you going to be my coach?"

Cy felt a laugh catch in his throat — not amusement, but something tender, something that made his chest tighten. He pulled Tom in even closer.

"Buddy," he said, "I'll always be your coach."

And he meant it in every way a father can mean it — on the field, off the field, and in all the places a boy grows up needing someone steady at his back.

THE GROUND BENEATH US

Over the next several months, as late summer turned to fall and eventually gave way to winter, Cy spent a few hours each week chipping away at his long to-do list for the league's first season. As promised to Joanne, he kept most of the work confined to weekends and made sure household chores didn't slip. He also carved out time for Tom, though the boy was spending more weekends with friends now — a natural shift for his age.

Meanwhile, Joe Muscovitz spoke to the Galesburg Chamber of Commerce and secured three additional team sponsors. Cy cashed in a few favors of his own and, while disappointed he couldn't convince more businesses to join, managed to add two more as well. That brought the total to six.

The inaugural season of the **Greater Galesburg Athletic Club** would feature:
- **The Wine Store Bears**
- **Amity Used Car Cougars**
- **Wagner Carpet Trojans**
- **Value Hardware Nationals**
- **Alter Street Café Chargers**
- **All-State Construction Oilers**

Most sponsors saw the advertising potential, but what truly motivated them was the same force driving Cy: the hope of one day beating Haleyville under the Friday night lights.

There was one exception. The owner of the Alter Street Café negotiated a set of brass bathroom fixtures in exchange for sponsorship — just before Cy finished his remodeling job there.

After researching typical sponsorship fees and negotiating with his backers, Cy settled on $400 per team. That fee guaranteed the sponsor's name on each jersey, signage at the field, and placement in game-day programs if they were printed. The championship trophy would also be displayed at the winning sponsor's business for a full year.

Cy divided the six teams into two conferences — National and American — and scheduled each team to play the others twice, creating a ten-week regular season. The top team from each conference would face off in week eleven for the G.G.A.C. League Championship. Ties would be broken first by head-to-head record, then by total points scored against the other team. If still tied, Cy figured he'd deal with it when the time came.

He documented all league rules in a booklet to be distributed during sign-ups.

As for the Pony and Midget divisions, Cy decided to wait a year or two. That would give Pee-Wee players time to develop before advancing. If he couldn't join a regional league for those divisions, he'd create a separate one for older players using the same structure he used for the Pee-Wee league.

Registration would begin in late June, with practices starting in July and games kicking off the first Saturday in September. The season would wrap up just before Thanksgiving — timed to avoid the worst of Pennsylvania's early winter.

One major challenge remained: recruiting nearly eighty players to fill six teams. Even with that number, most kids would have to play both offense and defense, with only a few extras to cover injuries or absences. Cy was determined to avoid forfeits.

He also spent the winter recruiting coaches. His goal was one experienced coach per team, supported by parent volunteers. Given the energy parents showed at Galesburg High games — often shouting advice at referees and coaches alike — Cy figured finding assistants wouldn't be hard.

By Valentine's Day, Cy had five head coaches lined up: himself, Stosh, and three others. But finding the sixth proved difficult. After nearly seven weeks of searching, he met Matt "Matty" Kelly while shopping for a used car for Joanne.

Matty was infamous in town — not for his salesmanship, but for leading the Galesburg High football team to a 0–19 record over two seasons. The town had tolerated mediocrity before, but that streak was enough to get him removed. Still, he had coaching experience. Despite his reputation for a hot temper and heavy drinking, Cy figured Matty was a workable final addition. Matty accepted without hesitation.

By early April, with most major tasks complete, Cy turned his attention to the fields. Though the site behind the town garage wasn't on his usual route home, he often detoured just to drive by — like a homebuyer imagining renovations. But now, with spring approaching, it was time to stop driving past and start walking the ground.

Late one Saturday afternoon, Cy grabbed a half-empty notebook, a sharpened pencil, and his old 110mm camera. The sun was high enough for photos but low enough to cast golden shadows across the cumulus clouds. The scene felt like a promise.

He didn't see weeds or litter. He saw six Pee-Wee teams practicing in the late summer sun. He heard whistles, cheers, and the crack of pads on a crisp fall Saturday. This place had a future.

Cy walked the entire property, noting elevation, pacing off dimensions, and taking photos. He mapped out six practice areas spaced to avoid interference and began evaluating spots for the main field. It needed to be level, large enough for regulation play, and close to parking, possible concessions, and — ideally — an electrical source. He had permission to use the town garage's employee lot when closed for parking, so he focused on placing the field nearby. Satisfied with his initial survey, he packed up and headed home.

The following Saturday, after developing his photos, Cy sketched the final layout. Fortunately, he found a section near the paved lot that was large enough for the main field and its supporting features. To fit six teams, two would share the main field at opposite ends. Two others would practice near a grove of widely spaced trees.

Next came clearing and grooming.

Joe Muscovitz had the equipment needed to clear weeds and prep the soil. Cy, Joe, Stosh, and two of Joe's employees spent an early spring Saturday transforming the site. By day's end, Cy was stunned by the progress. The next day, they tilled the ground.

During tilling, one of Joe's employees — Mike — stopped the machine when a large rock jammed the tines.

The stone was flecked with blue. Curious, Mike broke off a piece and pocketed it.

Later, as the crew packed up, Mike called out, "Hey Joe! Take a look at this — found it in the field."

Joe walked over. "Whatcha got?"

"A rock with blue specks. Ever seen anything like it?"

"How the hell should I know? I'm no geologist," Joe replied.

"Just thought it was odd."

"Maybe you can sell it to one of those rock hunters," Joe joked, walking away.

Mike tossed the rock aside and headed for his truck, reflecting on the weekend's work. The site was now fully prepped for seeding.

Since the town would benefit from the improved aesthetics, Cy convinced the council to split the cost of hiring a lawn care service to test the soil, seed, and fertilize the property. He'd cover the other half with sponsorship fees.

Cy asked around for reputable companies — ones that guaranteed results. After several calls, he found a local family-owned business that promised to survey the site the next day and provide a written guarantee. Cy agreed.

That evening, the company called back. They could meet the deadline and offered a surprisingly low estimate. Pleased, Cy visited their office the next day during lunch and paid the deposit. A technician would begin soil testing within days.

A few weeks later, after returning from a morning coal delivery, Cy found a message waiting for him.

"Please call McDermott Lawn Service at your earliest convenience," it read.

He pointed to the phone on Jill's desk. "May I?"

"Sure," she said.

Cy dialed the number.

"McDermott Lawn Service, this is Sam."

"Yeah, this is Cy Mozatta. I just got a message to call you."

"Thanks for getting back to me, Cy. I hope you don't mind — I got your work number from your wife. I figured this was important enough to reach you right away."

"No problem. Is something wrong?"

Sam's tone shifted. "We just got the results from your soil tests. There's a serious problem."

Cy's stomach tightened. "What kind of problem?"

"Well… arsenic, lead, heavy metals, and high levels of cyanide. It's bad, Cy. Really bad."

"Cyanide?" Cy's voice rose. "Isn't that poison?"

"Yes. Cyanide interferes with oxygen uptake in the body. Even small amounts can cause dizziness, headaches, nausea. In children, exposure — especially through skin contact — can be dangerous. And it's not just cyanide. The lead levels are high enough to affect neurological development. This site isn't safe."

Cy was silent.

"Did you notice any blue tint in the soil or strange odors?" Sam asked.

"Not really. But one of the guys mentioned a rock with blue specks."

"That's consistent with cyanide contamination," Sam said. "We're obligated to report this to the EPA."

Cy exhaled slowly. "Any idea how this happened?"

"Could be old industrial solvents, fuel runoff, metal cleaners. VOCs — volatile organic compounds — are common in places like garages. But the cyanide? That's serious. You need to stop everything."

"Thanks for the call, Sam. I'll come by for the test results and provide my final payment."

Cy hung up the phone and stood still for a moment, absorbing the weight of what he'd just heard. Then he turned to Jill, who had overheard enough to understand something was wrong.

"I'm so sorry, Cy," she said gently. "Is there anything I can do?"

"No… thanks. I'm not even sure what I can do," Cy replied, his voice distant.

He walked slowly back to the garage area, his stomach aching as if he'd been punched. The kind of punch that knocks the wind out of you and leaves you gasping for air, searching for something to hold onto.

Cy struggled through the rest of the workday, distracted and hollow. He left early and drove to the lawn care office to pick up the test results and pay his bill. Then, almost instinctively, he headed to the fields.

But this time, instead of imagining teams practicing and games being played, all Cy could see was an empty, poisoned landscape. The soil, once full of promise, now felt like a dormant threat — choked with toxins, waiting to harm anyone who came too close.

Standing there, Cy made a quiet vow: whoever was responsible for this contamination would be held accountable. He suspected the town garage, the only nearby structure, and considered the possibility that years of careless disposal had left the land tainted. During his time as a substitute driver, he hadn't seen anything suspicious — but that didn't mean it hadn't happened before.

Since the garage was still open, Cy decided to walk over and see if Paul Vittel was on site. He entered through a side door that led past Paul's office, but the room was empty. Continuing to the front desk, he spotted Lisa, one of the dispatchers, watering a large plant in the corner.

"Hey Lisa," Cy called out.

She turned and smiled. "Hi big guy! What brings you here?"

"Is Paul around? I need to talk to him right away." Cy held up the paper with the test results.

"He was, but he got called to Town Hall about an hour ago. Left in a hurry and looked upset. He's not in trouble, is he?"

"Don't think so… but someone is," Cy said. "Tell him to call me at home as soon as he can."

"Will do. I'll leave a note on his chair. Don't be a stranger," Lisa replied.

As Cy walked to his car, he figured McDermott's must have already contacted the EPA and the news had reached Paul. Why else would he rush to Town Hall?

Near his car, Cy noticed a faint blue tinge in the soil — something he hadn't seen before. It looked harmless, almost inviting. But now he knew better. And what if he hadn't hired a professional lawn service? What if he'd seeded the field himself? The thought was chilling.

Cy drove home, trying to shake the mood that had settled over him. He didn't want Joanne or Tom to feel the weight of his disappointment. He reminded himself of everything he'd accomplished and tried to believe there was still time to find a new site. He planned to inform the coaches and sponsors immediately, hoping one of them might have a solution.

When he arrived home, Joanne was at the kitchen table helping Tom with his homework.

"Hi honey," she said.

"Hey Dad," Tom added.

"Hi," Cy replied, his voice flat.

Joanne stood and took his coat. "Oh no, I know that tone. Rough day?"

"Got some bad news," Cy said. "Turns out the whole site around the town garage is contaminated. Soil test came back today. Just what I needed."

"Oh sweetie, I'm so sorry. Can they clean it up?"

"Not according to McDermott's. It's serious. They're calling the EPA. No short-term fix."

Cy sat down and placed his hand on Tom's. "Don't worry, buddy. I'll figure something out. We'll find another place to play."

"Can I help?" Tom offered. "Maybe I can ride my bike around town and look for a new place."

"Thanks, Tom. I'll let you know," Cy said, touched but trying not to lean too hard on his son's optimism.

Joanne stepped in. "Why don't you lie down for a while? I need to start dinner anyway. I'll make something special tonight to take your mind off things."

Cy nodded and headed to the living room. Before long, he was asleep on the sofa.

About twenty minutes later, the phone rang. It was Paul. Joanne tried to explain that Cy was sleeping, but Paul insisted she wake him — he had something important to discuss.

Cy came to quickly when he heard who it was.

"Hey Paul, I guess you got my message," he said.

"Yeah, I did. Sorry to wake you, but your little project has sent the entire town council into a panic," Paul said. "I assume you know what's going on? Of all the things that could've happened…"

"Yeah, I heard. It's not like I planned it," Cy replied. "What the hell have you guys been putting in the soil over there?"

"Let me be clear — I had nothing to do with this," Paul said firmly. "It must've happened before my time. The guy before me used to joke about how easy it was to dump stuff back then, but I never thought much of it. Anyway, the EPA's sending someone tomorrow. All hell's about to break loose."

"I don't know what to say, Paul. Maybe it's good I came along. If this stuff's in the groundwater, people need to know. And if it happened before your time, you should be off the hook."

"That's not the point," Paul said. "The council will blame me just because I offered the site. They're ignorant enough to think none of this would've come to light if I hadn't."

"Maybe they're upset because some of them know exactly what happened," Cy said. "But if that's the case, they'll be too busy answering to the EPA to worry about who uncovered it. I'll support you however I can. I've been around enough to know you had nothing to do with it."

Paul was still rattled, but he promised to keep Cy updated.

After the call, Cy phoned Joe Muscovitz to share the news. To his surprise, Joe wasn't shocked. It was as if he'd suspected something all along but hadn't wanted to say anything unless the site turned out clean. He even hinted that such contamination wasn't unusual in town — and admitted his own construction business hadn't always been environmentally careful.

Cy mentioned the blue specks. "Turns out that's a sign of cyanide in the soil."

"Cyanide? I thought it was just a blue rock," Joe said. "So what now?"

"That's why I'm calling," Cy said. "We need a new site. Got any ideas?"

"Nothing off the top of my head, but I'll ask around."

Cy thanked him and returned to the kitchen, updating Joanne on the conversation and the unsettling reality that there were likely other contaminated sites around town.

Over the next few weeks, Cy broke his rule about limiting league work during the week. He contacted every sponsor and coach. To his disappointment, none had a ready solution. Though people were searching, Cy felt anxious.

Days passed. Then weeks — and the league still had no home.

Occasionally, a promising lead would surface, but each time, some obstacle — ownership, zoning, liability — shut it down.

Cy spent lunch hours on the phone or driving around, scouting locations. When he found one that seemed viable, he'd track down the owner and pitch his plan, only to be turned away again and again. Some said they weren't interested. Others couldn't commit long-term. Most didn't want permanent structures like bleachers or goalposts on their land.

The search was exhausting. And at home, the strain was beginning to show.

THE SEARCH FOR SOLID GROUND

The next few weeks tested Cy in ways he hadn't anticipated. Every morning he woke with the same thought: find a field. And every night he went to bed with the same frustration: no luck today. The contamination crisis had spread through town faster than gossip at the barbershop. Everyone knew about the poisoned soil behind the town garage, and everyone had an opinion about how it happened — and who was to blame.

Cy tried to stay focused on solutions, but the weight of the setback pressed on him. He spent lunch hours driving through back roads, scanning open spaces, abandoned lots, and unused corners of farmland. He made phone calls, knocked on doors, and pitched his vision to anyone who would listen. But each time he thought he'd found a promising location, the answer came back the same: no long-term commitments, no permanent structures, no liability.

The league needed a home, not a temporary patch of grass.

At home, the strain was beginning to show. Joanne tried to be patient, but she could see the toll it was taking on him. Tom, sensing the tension, kept his distance more than usual. Cy hated that. He had promised himself — and them — that this dream wouldn't consume him. Yet here he was, letting the disappointment seep into every corner of his life.

One evening, after another fruitless day of searching, Cy sat at the kitchen table staring at a map of Galesburg and the surrounding townships. Joanne placed a cup of tea beside him.

"You're wearing yourself down," she said softly.

"I know," Cy replied, rubbing his temples. "But I can't let this fall apart. Not after everything we've done."

"You'll find something," she said. "Just… don't lose yourself in the process."

Cy nodded, but the truth was, he felt like he was already losing pieces of himself — hope, energy, confidence — one day at a time.

The next morning, Cy decided to widen his search beyond Galesburg. He drove through neighboring towns, scanning for open land, parks, unused school fields — anything that might work. He stopped at township offices, asked questions, filled out inquiry forms, and left his contact information everywhere he went.

Still nothing.

Time was running out and the pressure was suffocating. Registration was supposed to begin in June. Parents were already asking questions. Coaches were checking in. Sponsors wanted updates. And Cy had nothing to tell them except, "I'm working on it."

One afternoon, after another dead-end lead, Cy pulled into the parking lot of a small diner on the outskirts of town. He sat in his car for a moment, staring at the steering wheel, feeling the weight of the past months settle on him like a heavy coat.

He finally went inside and ordered a coffee. As he sat there, staring out the window, he wondered if he had been foolish to think he could pull this off. Maybe the universe was telling him something. Maybe this was too big, too complicated, too much for one man to carry.

But then he thought of Tom — of the way his son's eyes lit up when they talked about the league. He thought of the kids in town who had nothing to look forward to. He thought of the sponsors who believed in him, the coaches who had signed on, the hours of planning, the dreams he had sketched in his notebook.

He couldn't quit. Not yet.

That evening, Cy made a decision. If the perfect field didn't exist, he would find something imperfect and make it work. He would think creatively, push harder, ask more questions, knock on more doors. He would not let the league die before it even began.

He grabbed his notebook and began listing every possible location he hadn't checked yet — church properties, old industrial lots, unused corners of public parks, even private farmland that might be available for seasonal use. He wrote down names of people he could call, people who might know someone, people who owed him favors.

He wasn't giving up. Not now.

The next morning, Cy woke with a renewed sense of determination. He drove to the far edge of town, following a lead from one of the coaches about an old farm that had been sitting unused for years. The property was large, flat, and bordered by a line of tall pines. It wasn't perfect, but it had potential.

Cy parked his car and stepped out, walking the perimeter slowly. The soil looked healthy — dark, rich, and free of the blue tint that now haunted his memory. The land sloped gently but evenly. There was room for parking. And most importantly, it felt safe.

He stood there for a long moment, imagining the possibilities.

Then he headed back to his car, pulled out his notebook, and wrote down the owner's name from the mailbox.

It was a start.

And for the first time in weeks, Cy felt something he hadn't felt since before the contamination call.

Hope.

Cy woke the next morning with a sense of purpose he hadn't felt in weeks. The lead on the old farm property lingered in his mind like a faint light in a long tunnel. It wasn't a guarantee — not even close — but it was something. And something was more than he'd had in a long time.

He grabbed his notebook, the one that had become a second brain these past months, and flipped to the page where he'd written the landowner's name: Earl Whitman. Cy recognized the name vaguely — Whitman had owned a large dairy operation years ago before retiring. The farm had been mostly dormant since then, save for a few leased acres used for hay.

Cy drove out to the Whitman property again, this time with a more critical eye. The land was quiet, the kind of quiet that comes from years of disuse. The farmhouse sat far back from the road, its white paint faded to a soft gray. A rusted tractor rested near the barn like an old workhorse put out to pasture. The fields, though overgrown, were open and promising.

Cy stepped out of his car and walked the perimeter again, this time taking more deliberate notes. The soil looked healthy — dark, loamy, and free of discoloration. He knelt and sifted a handful through his fingers. It smelled like earth should: clean, organic, alive.

He stood and looked across the field, imagining the layout. Six practice areas. One main field. Parking along the tree line. Concessions near the entrance. It could work. It really could.

But first, he needed Earl Whitman to say yes.

Cy found Earl's number through a mutual acquaintance and called that afternoon. The phone rang several times before a gravelly voice answered.

"Yeah?"

"Mr. Whitman? This is Cy Mozatta. I was hoping to talk to you about your property on Old Mill Road."

A pause. "What about it?"

Cy took a breath. "I'm organizing a youth football league here in Galesburg. We lost our original field due to contamination issues, and I'm looking for a new site. I was hoping to speak with you about possibly using a portion of your land."

Another pause — longer this time.

"You the one who's been walking around out there?" Earl asked.

"Yes sir. Just trying to get a sense of the space."

"Well," Earl said, "I'm not against talking. But I don't make decisions over the phone. You want to discuss it, you come out here tomorrow morning. Nine o'clock."

"I'll be there," Cy said, relief and nerves mixing in his chest.

The next morning, Cy arrived ten minutes early. Earl Whitman was already outside, leaning against the barn with a mug of coffee. He was in his seventies, tall and wiry, with a face carved by years of sun and work.

"You're punctual," Earl said. "Good start."

Cy smiled. "Thank you for meeting with me."

"Walk with me," Earl said, pushing off the barn.

They walked the property in silence at first. Earl moved slowly but deliberately, his eyes scanning the land with the familiarity of someone who had known every inch of it for decades.

"You want to put kids out here?" Earl finally asked.

"Yes sir. Six teams. Pee-Wee level. Practices during the week, games on Saturdays."

"And you'd need to put up posts, lines, maybe some bleachers?"

"Yes. Nothing permanent without your approval. And we'd maintain the grounds."

Earl grunted. "I don't like commitments. Haven't since my wife passed. Land's easier when it's quiet."

Cy nodded. "I understand. But this league… it's important. Not just to me. To the kids. To the town."

Earl stopped walking and looked at him — really looked at him.

"You the one who helped that Gallagher boy years back?" he asked.

Cy blinked. "Bob Gallagher? Yes, sir. We went to school together."

"He told me once," Earl said. "Said you stood up for him when no one else would."

Cy wasn't sure what to say.

Earl turned back toward the field. "Town could use more men like that."

They walked a bit farther before Earl spoke again.

"I'll think about it," he said. "No promises. But I'll think."

It wasn't a yes. But it wasn't a no.

And for Cy, that was enough to keep hope alive.

That evening, Cy told Joanne and Tom about the meeting. Joanne listened carefully, her expression softening for the first time in days.

"That sounds promising," she said.

"It's something," Cy replied. "And right now, something feels like everything."

Tom grinned. "I hope he says yes. That place sounds cool."

Cy ruffled Tom's hair. "Me too, buddy."

As he sat down at the kitchen table later that night, Cy opened his notebook and wrote a single line at the top of a fresh page:

If the ground is good, the rest will follow.

He didn't know if Earl Whitman would say yes. He didn't know if the league would survive this setback. But for the first time since the contamination call, he felt the path forward — uncertain, winding, but real.

And he was ready to walk it.

The next few days moved slowly — painfully slowly. Cy thought about Earl's answer more often than he cared to admit, half-expecting Earl Whitman to call, half-dreading that he wouldn't. Every time the phone rang, Cy's heart jumped, only to sink again when it was a wrong number, a sponsor checking in, or a reminder from the hardware store about a sale he didn't care about.

He tried to stay busy. He worked his coal route. He helped Tom with homework. He fixed a leaky faucet Joanne had been reminding him about for weeks. But no matter what he did, his mind drifted back to the Whitman farm.

It was the first location that felt right since the contamination disaster. The land was open, healthy, and full of possibility. And Earl — gruff as he was — hadn't shut the door. He'd said he'd think about it. For Cy, that was enough to keep hope alive.

But hope had a way of turning into anxiety when left alone too long.

By Thursday, Cy couldn't take the waiting anymore. He drove out to the Whitman property again — not to bother Earl, but to look at the land one more time. He parked along the dirt road and stepped out, breathing in the cool air.

The field stretched out before him, a patchwork of browns and greens, dotted with early shoots of wild grass. The pines along the far edge swayed gently in the breeze. It was quiet, peaceful, and full of potential.

Cy walked the perimeter again, pacing off distances, imagining where the goalposts would go, where the parents would sit, where the kids would run drills. He could see it all so clearly it almost hurt.

He was halfway across the field when he heard a voice behind him.

"You're back again."

Cy turned to see Earl standing near the fence line, hands in his pockets, watching him with a mixture of curiosity and amusement.

"Sorry," Cy said. "I didn't mean to intrude. I just... needed to see it again."

Earl nodded slowly. "Figured as much."

They stood in silence for a moment, the wind rustling through the grass between them.

"You're serious about this league," Earl finally said.

"I am," Cy replied. "It's not just football. It's something this town needs. Something the kids need."

Earl studied him for a long moment. "You remind me of someone."

"Who's that?"

"My brother," Earl said. "Stubborn as a mule. Once he got an idea in his head, nothing could shake it loose."

Cy smiled faintly. "I'll take that as a compliment."

Earl grunted. "Depends on the day."

Another pause. Then Earl took a deep breath.

"I talked to my daughter," he said. "She handles most of the legal stuff now. Told her what you wanted to do."

Cy's heart thudded. "And?"

"She thinks it's a good idea," Earl said. "Says the land ought to be used for something that matters. Something that brings people together."

Cy swallowed hard. "So… does that mean — "

Earl held up a hand. "Don't get ahead of yourself. I'm willing to let you use the land. But there are conditions."

"Anything," Cy said quickly.

"You maintain it. You keep it clean. And if anything goes wrong — anything at all — you come to me first."

Cy nodded. "Absolutely. I can do all of that."

Earl extended his hand. "Then we have ourselves an agreement."

Cy stared at the hand for a moment, hardly believing it. Then he grasped it firmly.

"Thank you," he said, his voice thick. "You have no idea what this means."

"Oh, I think I do," Earl replied. "Now go on. You've got a football league to build."

Cy drove home with the windows down, letting the cool air wash over him. For the first time since the contamination call, he felt light — almost buoyant. He had a field. A real field. A safe field. A field with room to grow.

When he walked through the front door, Joanne looked up from the stove.

"Well?" she asked.

Cy grinned. "We've got a home."

Joanne let out a breath she'd been holding for days and wrapped her arms around him. Tom came running in from the living room.

"Dad? Did he say yes?"

"He did," Cy said, lifting his son off the ground in a hug. "We're back in business."

Tom whooped and pumped his fist in the air. Joanne laughed. And for the first time in weeks, the house felt warm again.

That night, after everyone had gone to bed, Cy sat at the kitchen table with his notebook open. He flipped to the page where he'd written Earl's name and underlined it twice.

Then he wrote:

Whitman Field — Future Home of the G.G.A.C.

He stared at the words for a long moment, letting them settle into reality.

Tomorrow, the work would begin again — calls to make, plans to adjust, coaches to update, sponsors to reassure. But tonight, Cy allowed himself to feel something he hadn't felt in far too long.

Pride.

And the quiet certainty that, despite everything, he was still on the right path.

CLEARING THE WAY

The next morning, Cy woke before dawn, the kind of early rise that came not from an alarm but from purpose. For the first time in weeks, he felt momentum again — real, tangible momentum. Whitman Field wasn't just a possibility anymore. It was the future home of the G.G.A.C., and Cy intended to treat it that way.

He grabbed his notebook, a thermos of coffee, and headed out. The sun was just beginning to rise as he pulled up to the property. The field was bathed in soft gold, the dew shimmering across the grass like a thin layer of frost. It felt like a fresh start.

Cy stepped out of his car and took a long breath. The air was crisp, clean, and carried none of the chemical tang he now associated with the old site. This land felt alive.

He walked the perimeter again, this time with a more confident stride. He paced off distances, marked rough boundaries with small flags he'd brought, and sketched out the layout in his notebook. The main field would sit near the tree line, where the ground was most level. The practice areas would fan out across the open space. Parking would run along the old gravel lane.

It wasn't perfect. But it was good. And good was enough to build something great.

By mid-morning, Cy was back home, energized. Joanne noticed immediately.

"You look lighter," she said.

"I feel lighter," Cy replied. "I'm heading over to see Earl again this afternoon. Want to make sure we're on the same page before I start bringing people out there."

Joanne smiled. "I'm proud of you, you know."

Cy paused, touched. "Thanks. I needed that."

That afternoon, Cy returned to the Whitman property. Earl was sitting on the porch, a newspaper folded beside him.

"You're back early," Earl said.

"Wanted to go over a few things," Cy replied. "Just to make sure we're aligned."

Earl nodded. "Come on up."

Cy sat on the porch steps and opened his notebook. "I've sketched out the layout. Nothing permanent yet — just ideas. Wanted to run it by you."

Earl took the notebook and studied the drawings. His eyes moved slowly, thoughtfully.

"You've put a lot of work into this," he said.

"I have," Cy replied. "But I want to make sure it works for you too."

Earl closed the notebook and handed it back. "It does. Just remember — this land has history. My family worked it for generations. I'm trusting you with it."

"I won't let you down," Cy said.

Earl nodded once. "Then you can start bringing your people out here. Just keep me informed."

Cy stood, feeling a surge of gratitude. "Thank you, Earl. Really."

Earl waved him off. "Go on now. You've got work to do."

Over the next few days, Cy contacted the coaches and sponsors, updating them on the new location. The reaction was overwhelmingly positive — relief mixed with excitement. Stosh offered to help measure and mark the fields. Joe volunteered equipment and manpower again. Even Matty Kelly, gruff as ever, said he'd swing by to "make sure the place wasn't a dump."

Cy took it all in stride. For the first time since the contamination disaster, he really felt like the league was moving forward again.

But the EPA investigation into the old site was just beginning.

One afternoon, as Cy was organizing notes, the phone rang. It was Paul.

"Cy, you got a minute?" Paul asked, his voice tight.

"Yeah, what's going on?"

"The EPA guy was here today. Took samples, asked questions, the whole nine yards."

"And?"

"And it's bad," Paul said. "Worse than we thought. They found cyanide compounds, lead concentrations way above safe limits, and traces of industrial solvents that haven't been used legally in decades."

Cy felt a chill. "Any idea how long it's been there?"

"EPA thinks some of it dates back thirty, maybe forty years," Paul said. "Before my time. Before yours. Before half the council was even out of diapers."

Cy leaned back in his chair. "So what happens now?"

"They're going to expand the testing area," Paul said. "Check groundwater, nearby properties. This could turn into a full-scale remediation project."

Cy exhaled slowly. "I'm sorry, Paul. I didn't mean for any of this to blow up like it did."

"Don't apologize," Paul said. "If anything, you did the town a favor. If kids had been playing out there…" His voice trailed off.

Cy didn't need him to finish the sentence.

"Keep me posted," Cy said.

"I will," Paul replied. "And Cy… thanks for standing by me."

"Always," Cy said.

That evening, Cy sat at the kitchen table, staring at the test results he'd picked up from McDermott's. The numbers were stark — levels of contaminants far beyond anything safe. The blue flecks Mike had found were likely ferrocyanide compounds, often used decades ago in industrial processes. When exposed to sunlight and certain conditions, they could break down and release free cyanide.

It was a miracle no one had been hurt.

Joanne placed a hand on his shoulder. "You okay?"

"Yeah," Cy said quietly. "Just thinking how close we came."

Joanne squeezed his shoulder. "But you didn't. You caught it. And now you've got a new field. A better one."

Cy nodded. "Yeah. We do."

He closed the folder and set it aside.

Tomorrow, he would meet the coaches at Whitman Field. They would walk the land together, plan the layout, and begin the next phase of building the league.

For now, he allowed himself a moment of stillness.

The ground beneath him was solid again.

And the dream was alive.

The following Saturday, Cy stood at the edge of Whitman Field with a clipboard in hand and a fresh set of stakes tucked under his arm. The coaches had arrived one by one, each bringing a mix of curiosity, skepticism, and quiet hope. Stosh was already pacing the perimeter, measuring strides and muttering about drainage. Matty Kelly leaned against his truck, arms crossed, watching the others with his usual guarded expression.

Cy gathered them near the tree line and began outlining the plan. He pointed to the flagged areas, described the layout, and explained how the teams would rotate through practice zones. The main field would sit closest to the gravel lane, with enough space for bleachers, concessions, and parking.

"It's not perfect," Cy admitted. "But it's ours. And it's clean."

The men nodded. No one needed reminding of the contamination disaster. It lingered in the background like a bruise — visible, painful, but healing.

Joe Muscovitz arrived last, hauling a trailer of equipment behind his truck. He stepped out, surveyed the field, and gave a low whistle.

"You weren't kidding," he said. "This place has potential."

Cy smiled. "Let's make it real."

The rest of the day was spent marking boundaries, measuring dimensions, and clearing brush. Joe's crew brought out a small bulldozer and a brush cutter, and by mid-afternoon, the field had begun to take shape. The tall grass was gone. The practice zones were defined. The main field was roughed in.

Cy worked nonstop, sweat soaking through his shirt, hands blistered from hammering stakes and dragging fencing. But he didn't care. Every swing of the mallet, every line drawn in the dirt, felt like progress.

By sunset, the group stood at the edge of the field, surveying their work. It wasn't finished — not even close — but it was real. Tangible. Alive.

"We'll need to seed soon," Stosh said. "And get those goalposts up."

"I'll handle the posts," Joe offered. "Got some old pipe we can weld."

Cy nodded. "Let's meet again next weekend. We'll keep pushing."

The men dispersed, leaving Cy alone at the field. He walked the perimeter one last time, the sky streaked with orange and purple above him. He paused near the fence, looking out over the land.

It was happening.

But not everything was moving forward.

The EPA investigation had expanded. Paul called Cy midweek with an update.

"They've found traces of contamination in the groundwater," Paul said. "Not just cyanide — benzene, toluene, even some PCBs."

Cy felt his stomach drop. "That's industrial-grade stuff."

"Exactly," Paul said. "They think it came from illegal dumping back in the '40s. Solvents, degreasers, maybe even battery acid. The garage was used for all kinds of things back then."

"Is it spreading?"

"They're not sure yet," Paul replied. "But they've cordoned off the area. No one's allowed within fifty feet of the original site."

Cy exhaled. "What about liability?"

"That's the problem," Paul said. "The town council's panicking. They're worried about lawsuits, property values, public health. And some of them are pointing fingers — at me, at you, at anyone who touched the site."

Cy clenched his jaw. "We didn't cause this."

"I know," Paul said. "But politics doesn't care about truth. It cares about optics."

Cy was silent.

"They're holding a closed-door meeting next week," Paul added. "I'm not invited. But you can bet your name's going to come up."

Cy felt the old frustration rising. He had done everything right. He had followed the rules, asked permission, taken precautions. And now, because he'd uncovered a decades-old mess, he was being treated like a liability.

"I'll be there," Cy said. "They don't get to talk about me without me."

That night, Cy sat at the kitchen table with Joanne, explaining the situation.

"They're scared," he said. "And when people get scared, they look for someone to blame."

Joanne listened quietly, then reached for his hand.

"You didn't do anything wrong," she said. "You did something good. You protected those kids. You exposed something dangerous. That matters."

Cy nodded. "I just hope they see it that way."

Joanne squeezed his hand. "If they don't, we'll remind them."

The next morning, Cy returned to Whitman Field. He walked the land slowly, checking the stakes, inspecting the soil, imagining the games that would one day be played here.

He paused near the fence and looked out over the field.

Whatever happened at Town Hall, whatever politics tried to twist, this place was real. It was clean. It was safe.

And it was waiting.

The closed-door meeting at Town Hall was scheduled for Tuesday evening. Cy arrived early, dressed in his cleanest work shirt and carrying a folder of documents — soil reports, league plans, sponsor letters. He wasn't invited, but he wasn't going to be ignored either.

Paul met him on the steps. "They're nervous," he said. "But I think they're ready to listen."

Inside, the council members sat around a long oak table, their expressions guarded. Cy stood at the end, waiting for someone to acknowledge him.

Mayor Hensley finally spoke. "Mr. Mozatta, we didn't expect you."

"I figured," Cy replied. "But I'm here anyway."

He placed the folder on the table. "I didn't cause the contamination. But I did uncover it. And I'm not sorry. If kids had played on that field, we'd be talking about hospital visits, not football games."

A few council members shifted uncomfortably.

"I've moved the league to a clean site. I've got sponsors, coaches, and kids ready to play. All I need is for this town to stop treating me like a problem and start seeing me as part of the solution."

Silence.

Then Councilwoman Dillard cleared her throat. "The EPA confirmed the contamination predates current operations. They're handling cleanup. Liability falls on the state, not the town."

Cy nodded. "Then let's move forward."

Mayor Hensley leaned back. "You have our support. Officially."

Cy exhaled. "Thank you."

By the weekend, Whitman Field was buzzing with activity. Joe's crew returned with fresh gravel for the parking area. Stosh oversaw the installation of goalposts, barking orders like a seasoned foreman. Matty Kelly showed up with a truckload of cones and field markers, surprising everyone — including himself.

Cy stood near the edge of the field, watching it all unfold. The grass was coming in strong, thanks to the early seeding and favorable weather. The practice zones were marked. The main field was lined. Bleachers were being assembled from salvaged lumber donated by a local contractor.

It was happening.

Joanne and Tom arrived mid-afternoon, carrying sandwiches and lemonade for the crew. Tom ran off to help measure yard lines, while Joanne joined Cy at the fence.

"It's beautiful," she said.

"It's real," Cy replied.

That evening, Cy walked the field alone. The sun dipped low, casting long shadows across the grass. He paused at midfield, looking toward the goalposts, imagining the roar of the crowd, the squeal of whistles, the thud of helmets.

He knelt and pressed his hand to the turf.

It was firm. It was clean.

It was ready.

A TOWN BELIEVES

Momentum didn't just build — it rolled through Galesburg like a quiet tide. Once Whitman Field was declared clean and people saw the progress, something shifted in the town. People who had barely spoken to Cy before were suddenly reaching out, curious, hopeful, eager to be part of something that felt new.

The first calls came from parents he recognized from the grocery store or school pickup lines. Then came names he didn't know — families from the far end of town, parents who worked double shifts, grandparents raising grandkids, people who had never had the time or resources to get their children into organized sports. Their voices carried a mix of relief and longing.

"My son needs something positive after school. He's been struggling since the divorce."

"My son's been begging for a team to join. He's fast — really fast."

"We've needed this for years. Thank you for doing it."

Cy listened to every story, jotting down names, ages, and questions in a notebook that was quickly filling with scribbles. Each call reinforced what he already knew: this league wasn't just a pastime — it was a lifeline.

At home, Tom's excitement grew by the hour. He hovered around Cy like a shadow, firing off questions faster than Cy could answer them.

"Will we have real uniforms?" "What about team names?" "Can I play quarterback?" "When do practices start?" "Do we get helmets with stripes?"

Cy laughed more in those days than he had in months. "We'll figure it out," he kept saying, even though he was still sorting through half the logistics himself. But Tom's enthusiasm — pure, unfiltered, and relentless — reminded him why he had started this journey in the first place. It wasn't about football. It was about giving kids a place to belong.

One evening, Cy sat at the kitchen table surrounded by papers — practice schedules, equipment lists, volunteer forms, budget notes. Joanne joined him, carrying two mugs of tea. She set one beside him — Earl Grey with milk and sugar, his favorite — and leaned over his shoulder, scanning the growing stack.

"You're really making progress," she said, her voice warm.

"I hope so," Cy replied. "There's still a lot to figure out, but people are starting to believe in it."

"They believe in you," she said gently.

Cy paused, struck by the sincerity in her tone. Joanne had been there through every setback — the contamination scare, the long nights of doubt. She had listened when he vented, encouraged him when he faltered, and celebrated every small victory. Her belief had become a quiet source of strength.

As the night wore on, Cy continued planning. He refined age groups, drafted a tentative game schedule, and made notes about equipment needs. He knew the road ahead would be challenging, but he also knew he wasn't walking it alone. The community was beginning to rally behind him, and with each passing day, the dream of a youth football league in Galesburg felt less like a gamble and more like a promise.

For the first time, he allowed himself to imagine the moment the league would officially begin: kids in uniforms sprinting across the field, parents cheering from the sidelines, the smell of fresh-cut grass, the crackle of a loudspeaker announcing the start of the season. The thought filled him with a sense of purpose he hadn't felt in years.

As weeks passed, the support only grew. Parents called regularly to ask about registration, practice schedules, and equipment. Some volunteered to coach. Others offered to help with snacks, carpools, or fundraising. A few even donated old gear their kids had outgrown. Cy kept meticulous notes, determined not to let anything slip through the cracks.

Then came the call from the elementary school principal.

"Mr. Mozatta," the principal said, "I've heard a lot of positive things about your youth football league. I'd like to offer the school gym for registration night if you need a space."

Cy blinked, surprised and grateful. "That would be perfect. Thank you."

"Happy to help," the principal replied. "This is exactly the kind of program our kids need."

With a location secured, Cy threw himself into preparations. He created flyers, drafted sign-up sheets, and coordinated volunteers to help manage the crowd. He wanted the event to run smoothly — not just to make a good impression, but to show the community that the league was organized, dependable, and here to stay.

Registration night exceeded every expectation.

Families streamed through the gym doors, their voices echoing off the polished floor. Kids ran excitedly between tables, their sneakers squeaking across the varnished wood. Parents filled out forms, asked questions, and chatted with volunteers. Some brought younger siblings who toddled around clutching juice boxes. Others arrived straight from work, still in uniforms or scrubs, grateful for something hopeful to look forward to.

By the end of the evening, almost a hundred children had signed up.

As Cy gathered the last of the forms, he felt a mixture of pride and disbelief. What had started as a simple idea — a hope, really — was becoming something far greater. The community had embraced the league, and the children were eager to begin.

Over the next few days, Cy worked tirelessly to sort the registration forms, organize players into age groups, and assign them to teams. He contacted volunteer coaches and scheduled practices. Each task brought the league closer to its official launch.

One evening, Tom watched him from the doorway, his eyes bright.

"Dad," he said, "I can't believe how many kids signed up."

"Me neither," Cy said with a smile. "It's amazing what can happen when people come together."

Tom nodded thoughtfully. "I'm glad you didn't give up."

Cy looked at his son, feeling a swell of emotion. "Me too," he said. "This is for you, you know. And for every kid who wants a chance to play."

Cy woke before dawn that following Saturday, long before his alarm buzzed. The house was quiet, the kind of stillness that only existed before the world remembered it had things to do. He lay there for a moment, staring at the ceiling, letting the weight of the past few weeks settle into something real. Not hope. Not fear. Something steadier.

Responsibility.

He swung his legs out of bed, careful not to wake Tom, and padded into the kitchen. The coffee pot sputtered to life, filling the room with a warm, earthy smell. As he waited, he glanced at the stack of registration forms spread across the table — color-coded, sorted, and clipped into neat piles. Ninety-seven kids. Ninety-seven families who had trusted him with their children.

He felt that weight too. And he welcomed it.

By the time he reached Whitman Field, the sun was just beginning to rise, casting a soft orange glow across the grass. Cy unlocked the small equipment shed and began hauling out gear — cones, footballs, practice jerseys — setting them in tidy rows along the sideline.

He wasn't expecting anyone this early, so the sound of tires crunching over gravel caught him off guard.

A silver sedan pulled in. The door opened, and out stepped Mrs. Alvarez, a woman Cy recognized from registration night. Her son, Mateo, had been one of the first to sign up — quiet kid, big eyes, nervous smile.

"Morning, Mr. Mozatta," she called, waving.

"Morning," Cy replied. "Everything alright?"

She approached with a shy smile. "I just wanted to drop off these." She held out a box filled with neatly folded towels, water bottles, and a few unopened packs of athletic tape. "I work at the hospital. We had extras. I thought the kids might need them. I was going to leave them here with a note but I'm glad I ran into you."

Cy blinked, touched. "This is… more than generous."

She shrugged. "My boy hasn't stopped talking about this league. He's never been excited about anything before. So… thank you."

Before Cy could respond, another car pulled in. Then a truck. Then two more. Parents stepped out carrying donations — coolers, first-aid kits, old cleats, even a portable scoreboard someone had salvaged from a storage unit.

Cy stood there, stunned, as the small procession formed an impromptu line that had clearly been coordinated.

"We figured you could use this." "Thought the league might need a few extras." "My brother's company had these lying around." "Coach, you're doing something good. Let us help."

Cy swallowed hard. He hadn't asked for any of this. But the town had decided to give anyway.

By mid-morning, the sideline looked like a miniature equipment warehouse. Stosh arrived, took one look, and let out a low whistle.

"Looks like Christmas came early."

Cy exhaled a laugh. "I don't even know where to put all this."

"Good problem to have," Stosh said, clapping him on the shoulder.

As they sorted through the donations, a familiar voice called out from behind them.

"Dad!"

Tom sprinted across the field, Joanne trailing behind him with a smile.

"You should've seen it at the store," Tom said breathlessly. "Everyone's talking about the league. Everyone."

Cy raised an eyebrow.

Joanne stepped closer. "It's spreading, Cy. People are excited. Really excited."

Cy looked around — at the parents unloading supplies, at the volunteers organizing each item, at the kids who had started tossing a football around even though practice hadn't officially begun.

The league wasn't just forming.

It was taking root.

Later that afternoon, Cy met with the volunteer coaches in the community center. They gathered around a long folding table, clipboards in hand, ready to talk schedules, drills, safety protocols, and team assignments. Some were former high school players. Some were dads who had never coached anything before. One was a retired Marine who had already offered to run conditioning drills.

Cy walked them through the plan — practice rotations, age brackets, equipment distribution, and the tentative game schedule. The coaches asked thoughtful questions, offered suggestions, and took notes like they were preparing for a championship season.

When the meeting ended, Coach Stosh lingered.

"You know," he said, "I've seen a lot of things in my time. But this?" He gestured toward the door, where the muffled sound of kids laughing drifted in from outside. "This is different."

Cy nodded. "It is."

"You ready for what comes next?" Stosh asked.

Cy thought about the field, the kids, the parents, the donations, the registration night, the coaches, the long nights at the kitchen table.

"Yeah," he said quietly. "I think I am."

Stosh grinned. "Good. Because the first official practice is in three days. And something tells me it's gonna be big."

Cy smiled back, a slow, steady smile that came from somewhere deep.

Three days.

Three days until the dream became real.

THE WHISTLE THAT STARTED
IT ALL

The first official practice was scheduled for an early Tuesday evening in mid-July. Cy arrived at Whitman Field more than an hour early. The grass was still damp from a recent shower, and the sky held that pale blue hue that only came with the haze of summer humidity. He moved quietly, setting out cones, arranging footballs in neat rows, and reviewing the practice plan he'd drafted the night before. His clipboard was worn, corners curled, but the notes were clear. Today mattered.

He paused at midfield, scanning the empty field. The goalposts stood tall, the lines freshly chalked. It looked like a real football field now — not a patch of reclaimed dirt, not a dream. Something solid. Something earned.

As the sun continued its early evening journey, cars began to pull into the gravel lot. Families emerged slowly — some still recovering from the day's work, others already buzzing with energy. Boys spilled out of back seats and truck beds, some wearing oversized cleats and others hand-me-down practice jerseys. Their voices filled the air with laughter, nervous chatter, and the occasional shout of recognition.

Parents gathered along the sidelines, folding chairs in hand, drink cups in hand. They chatted with one another, watched their sons warm up, and exchanged stories about the league's formation. Cy greeted each family with a smile, shaking hands, answering questions, and offering quiet reassurance. He could feel their eyes on him — not with skepticism, but with hope.

When all the players had arrived, Cy blew his whistle. The sharp sound cut through the air, and the boys hustled toward him, forming a loose semicircle at midfield. Their faces were bright with curiosity — some serious, others barely containing their excitement.

Cy took a moment to look at them — dozens of boys   from   different   neighborhoods,   different backgrounds, all united by their eagerness to play. It was a sight he knew he would never forget.

"Welcome to the first day of the Galesburg Youth Football League," he began, voice steady. "I'm proud of each of you for being here. Today, we're going to learn the basics — how to work together, how to listen, how to give your best effort. Football is about more than winning. It's about teamwork, discipline, and respect. If you give your best, you'll get better every day."

The boys nodded. Some stood tall, others fidgeted, but all were listening.

Cy introduced the volunteer coaches — local dads, uncles, and a retired gym teacher who had offered to help. He assigned players to their teams and explained the practice schedule. Then he blew his whistle again, and the field erupted into motion.

Children ran drills, practiced handoffs, and learned how to line up properly. Coaches shouted encouragement. Parents clapped from the sidelines. The sound of laughter and thudding footsteps filled the air, creating a rhythm that felt like the heartbeat of something new.

Cy moved from group to group, offering guidance and support. He knelt to adjust a boy's stance, demonstrated a proper snap, and reminded one group to stay light on their feet. With every correction came a smile, a nod, a moment of connection. This was what he had imagined during those early days in the grocery store parking lot. This was the dream he had fought to bring to life.

Tom threw himself into the drills with enthusiasm. Cy watched him from a distance, feeling a sense of pride. Tom wasn't the biggest or the fastest, but he listened carefully, worked hard, and encouraged his teammates. Cy saw in him the same love for the game that he had felt as a boy, tossing a football with his father in their backyard.

As practice drew to a close, Cy gathered the players once more.

"Great work today," he said. "This is just the beginning. Keep showing up, keep trying your best, and you'll be amazed at what you can accomplish."

The boys cheered, their faces flushed with effort and joy. Parents clapped. Coaches exchanged satisfied nods. Several families approached Cy to thank him personally. Their words were simple, but their gratitude was profound.

When the field finally emptied, Cy stood alone for a moment, taking it all in. The sun was beginning to set, casting a warm glow across the grass. He felt tired, but it was the kind of tired that came from doing something meaningful. Something that mattered.

He gathered the equipment and took one last look at the field.

The league had officially begun.

And with it, a new chapter for the boys of Galesburg.

In the weeks that followed, the league settled into a rhythm. Practices evolved from simple tag tackles to full knock-down tackles after the league equipment finally arrived.

When youth football players suit up in full gear for the first time, the transformation is striking. Helmets wobble slightly on heads still growing into them, shoulder pads jut out like armor borrowed from older brothers, and jerseys hang loose over skinny frames. From a distance, they look like miniature gladiators — tough, battle-ready, and serious. But up close, they're still just kids: wide-eyed, grinning, adjusting chin straps with nervous fingers, and sneaking glances at their parents for reassurance. The gear might make them look fierce, but beneath it all are boys chasing a dream, learning the game, and discovering what it means to be part of something bigger than themselves.

Practices were held three evenings a week, and the field — once quiet and underused — now buzzed with activity. The sound of whistles, laughter, and pounding pads filled the air, creating a kind of music that echoed across the neighborhood.

Coaches grew more confident. Players began to grasp the fundamentals. Parents adapted to the routine — drop-offs, pickups, sideline chats. Some even stayed to help, setting up cones or handing out water bottles.

Cy made it a point to visit each group during practice. He watched as boys who had never played football before began to understand the game — how to hold the ball, how to block, how to trust one another. He saw shy boys gain confidence, energetic boys learn discipline, and teammates form friendships that spilled over into school hallways and weekend hangouts.

Each small improvement felt like a victory. Not just for the players, but for the town.

One evening, as Cy walked from one field to another, he overheard a group of parents talking.

"I can't believe how much my son loves this," one mother said. "He's never been this excited about anything before."

Another nodded. "It's good for them. Gives them something to look forward to. Something positive."

Cy didn't interrupt. He just smiled and kept walking, their words settling into his chest like warmth.

Tom continued to thrive. He practiced diligently, listened to his coaches, and encouraged his teammates. Cy watched him grow — not just as a player, but as a young man. He saw the determination in Tom's eyes, the way he pushed himself to improve, and the joy he felt when he succeeded.

It was everything Cy had hoped for.

As the season progressed, Cy began preparing for the league's first official games. He coordinated with coaches to finalize schedules, arranged for referees, and worked with volunteers to set up concessions and manage the crowds. The amount of work was overwhelming at times, but Cy approached each task with quiet determination.

He knew the success of the league depended on planning, and he was committed to making the experience memorable.

The night before the first game, Cy stood alone on the main field. The lines were freshly painted. Yard markers stood in place. The setting sun cast a soft glow across the grass, and the quiet of the evening felt almost sacred.

He thought about everything that had led to this moment — the disappointment in Haleyville, the spark of inspiration in the grocery store parking lot, the long nights, the setbacks, the support.

For a moment, he allowed himself to feel the full weight of what he had accomplished.

The league was no longer just an idea.

It was real.

It was alive.

And tomorrow, the boys of Galesburg would take the field for the first time — ready to play, to learn, and to grow.

As he turned to leave, Cy felt a deep sense of gratitude. For the community. For the volunteers. For Joanne and Tom. And for the chance to make a difference in a place that needed hope.

The journey was far from over.

But the foundation had been laid.

And the future, for the first time in a long while, felt bright.

In fact, the future arrived sooner than Cy expected.

SATURDAYS IN GALESBURG

Game day arrived with a sense of anticipation that seemed to ripple through the entire town. Long before the first whistle, families began gathering at the field, carrying folding chairs, blankets, and thermoses of coffee. Children in oversized equipment ran across the grass, their excitement contagious. The air was cool but pleasant — the kind of late-summer morning that made everything feel fresh and full of possibility.

Cy arrived early, as he always did, to make sure everything was ready. He checked the field markings, tested the scoreboard, and spoke with the referees to confirm the rules and schedule. As he worked, he felt a mixture of nerves and pride. This was the moment he had imagined countless times — the moment when the league would truly come alive, when the children of Galesburg would take the field not just to practice, but to compete.

As the stands filled, Cy walked along the sidelines, greeting parents and answering last-minute questions. Many thanked him for his hard work, expressing gratitude for the opportunity he had created for their children. Cy accepted their thanks humbly, knowing the league belonged to the entire community, not just to him.

When it was time for the first game to begin, Cy gathered the players at midfield. The children stood in two neat lines, their helmets gleaming in the morning sun. Some looked nervous, others eager, but all of them were ready. Cy took a moment to look at their faces, feeling a surge of emotion. This was why he had fought so hard. This was the dream made real.

"Today is a special day," Cy said, his voice carrying across the field. "You've all worked hard to get here. Remember what you've learned — teamwork, effort, respect. Play your best, support your teammates, and have fun. That's what this league is all about."

The players nodded, and the crowd applauded. Cy stepped back as the referees signaled for the game to begin. The first kickoff soared through the air, and the field erupted into motion. Parents cheered, coaches shouted instructions, and the players threw themselves into the game with enthusiasm and determination.

As Cy watched from the sidelines, he felt a deep sense of fulfillment. The children were learning, growing, and discovering the joy of competition. The parents were engaged, cheering loudly and proudly. The community had come together in a way he hadn't seen in years. It was everything he had hoped for — and more.

Tom played with heart, making several good tackles and encouraging his teammates after every play. Cy watched him closely, feeling both pride and gratitude. Seeing his son out there, part of something bigger than himself, made every challenge along the way worthwhile.

The games were all close, filled with moments of excitement and suspense. But it didn't really matter who won or lost. When the final whistle blew for the last game of the day, the teams shook hands, their faces flushed with effort and pride. The crowd applauded, celebrating not just the outcome but the effort, the sportsmanship, and the spirit of the league.

As families began to pack up and head home, many stopped to thank Cy again. Some offered to volunteer more, others asked how they could help with future games. The sense of community was palpable, and Cy felt humbled by the outpouring of support.

When the field finally cleared, Cy stood alone for a moment, taking in the quiet as he often did. The grass was worn in places, the yard lines slightly smudged, but to him, it looked perfect. It was a field that had seen the beginning of something important — something that would shape the lives of countless children for years to come.

He gathered the remaining equipment, loaded it into his car, and took one last look at the field before heading home. The league had taken its first step, and it had been a success. And Cy knew, deep in his heart, that this was only the beginning.

In the weeks that followed the first game, the league continued to grow in ways Cy had never imagined. Each Saturday brought larger crowds, louder cheers, and a stronger sense of community. Families who rarely interacted before now stood side by side on the sidelines, sharing stories, offering encouragement, and celebrating the small victories of children they had only recently met. The league had become more than a sports program — it had become a gathering place, a source of pride, and a reminder of what the town could accomplish when it came together.

Cy found himself busier than ever. Between organizing schedules, coordinating volunteers, and ensuring every team had the equipment they needed, his days were full. But despite the long hours, he felt energized. Every challenge he faced — whether it was a last-minute schedule change or a shortage of mouthguards — felt manageable because he knew the purpose behind it. He had created something meaningful, something that mattered to the children and families of Galesburg.

One afternoon, after a particularly exciting game, a group of parents approached Cy.

"We just wanted to thank you," one mother said. "My son has never been this confident. He talks about football nonstop."

Another nodded. "This league has changed our evenings and weekends. Instead of sitting inside, we're out here cheering and meeting new people. It's brought the town together."

Cy felt humbled by their words. "I'm glad it's making a difference," he said. "That's what this was all about."

As the parents walked away, Tom ran toward him, his face flushed with excitement.

"Dad! Did you see my tackle?"

"I sure did," Cy said, smiling. "You played great today."

Tom beamed, and Cy felt an upwelling of emotion. Watching his son grow — both as a player and as a person — made every moment of effort worthwhile.

Later that evening, Cy felt a renewed sense of purpose. The league was no longer just a dream. It was a living, breathing part of the community. And he was ready to guide it into whatever came next.

As the season progressed, the league became a fixture in the community. Saturday mornings were no longer quiet in Galesburg; instead, they were filled with the sounds of cheering parents and excited children. Cy continued to oversee every detail, ensuring the fields were ready, the equipment organized, and the volunteers prepared. He moved from game to game, offering encouragement to players and support to coaches. Though the work was demanding, he felt a deep sense of satisfaction. The league had grown beyond his expectations, and seeing the joy it brought to the children made every long day worthwhile.

On one particular Saturday, the weather had produced off-and-on showers, and Cy noticed an older man standing alone near the edge of the field holding an umbrella. The man watched the children intently, one hand tucked into the pocket of a worn jacket. Curious, Cy approached him.

"Enjoying the game?" he asked.

The man nodded slowly. "I am. Haven't seen this kind of excitement in Galesburg in a long time."

Cy smiled. "It's been great for the kids. And for the town."

The man looked at him thoughtfully. "You're the one who started all this, aren't you?"

Cy hesitated, modest as always. "I had the idea, but it's the community that made it happen."

The man chuckled softly. "Ideas like this don't come around often. You've given these kids something to be proud of. That matters."

Cy thanked him, touched by the unexpected praise. As the man walked away, Cy reminded himself that moments like that were why he had fought so hard to bring the league to life.

As the season neared its end, the excitement only grew. Parents talked about the upcoming championship games, children practiced plays in their neighborhoods, and coaches worked tirelessly to prepare their teams. The league had become more than a pastime — it had become a source of pride, a symbol of hope, and a reminder that even in a town shaped by hardship, good things could still take root.

At home, Tom's enthusiasm was stronger than ever. He practiced in the yard every evening, running drills and perfecting his footwork. Cy watched him with pride, seeing not just a young athlete but a boy growing in confidence and character. The league had given Tom something to strive for, something that made him feel capable and strong.

One evening, as Cy sat at the kitchen table reviewing notes for the final games, Joanne placed a hand on his shoulder.

"You've done something incredible," she said softly. "Look at what this league has become."

Cy glanced at the stack of papers — schedules, rosters, volunteer lists — and felt a flood of emotion. "It's been a lot of work," he admitted, "but seeing the kids out there… it makes everything worth it."

Joanne smiled. "You've changed this town, Cy. Don't forget that."

As the season approached its final weeks, Cy felt both excitement and a hint of sadness. The league had become such a central part of his life that he couldn't imagine Saturdays without it. But he also knew this was only the beginning. There would be more seasons, more players, and more opportunities to build something lasting.

As the final weeks of the season progressed, excitement in Galesburg reached a level Cy had never seen before. The upcoming championship games had become the talk of the town. At the grocery store, at the gas station, even at the mine, people discussed which teams looked strongest, which players had improved the most, and how proud they were of the children who had taken the field each week. The league had become a unifying force — something that brought people together regardless of their backgrounds or daily struggles.

Cy felt the weight of the season's end approaching. He wanted the final games to be memorable, not just for the players but for the entire community. He spent hours planning the event — organizing volunteers, arranging for extra seating, and doing everything he could to ensure the day ran smoothly. He wanted the children to feel celebrated, to understand how much their hard work and dedication meant.

One evening, as Cy reviewed the final game schedule, Tom approached him with a serious expression.

"Dad," he said, "do you think I'll win the championship?"

Cy looked at his son, seeing both hope and nerves in his eyes. "I think you and your team have worked hard," he said. "But winning isn't the only thing that matters. What matters is how you play — how you support your teammates, how you give your best, how you carry yourself. If you do that, you've already won."

Tom nodded slowly, absorbing his father's words. "I'll try my best."

"I know you will," Cy said, placing a hand on his shoulder.

As the championship day drew closer, the energy in the town grew stronger. Families even decorated their cars with team colors. Everyone looked forward to the final games of the season.

THE GAME THAT MADE A TOWN WHOLE

On the morning of the championship, Cy arrived at the field just before sunrise. The sky was still a deep blue, the kind that made the streetlights look brighter than they were. A thin layer of frost clung to the grass, sparkling faintly beneath the glow. Cy breathed in the cold air, feeling it settle in his chest like a reminder of how far the season had come.

He walked the length of the field slowly, hands tucked into his jacket pockets. He checked the lines, the goalposts, the seating — every detail mattered today. This wasn't just another Saturday. This was the culmination of months of effort, months of planning, organizing, and believing. He paused near midfield, letting his eyes sweep across the quiet expanse. In a few hours, this place would be alive.

As the sun began to rise, the frost softened, and the field took on a warm golden glow. Later that morning, cars started pulling into the lot. Families bundled in jackets and hats made their way toward the bleachers. The stands filled quickly, buzzing with anticipation. Children in their uniforms gathered near the sidelines, their faces a mix of determination and excitement. Coaches offered last-minute encouragement, parents snapped photos, and referees checked their whistles and flags.

Cy stood at midfield again, but this time the field pulsed with life. The league — once just an idea he scribbled on a notepad — had grown into something far greater than he ever imagined. It had given the children of Galesburg a place to grow, to learn, and to believe in themselves. And it had given the town a reason to come together, to cheer, and to hope.

As the first game approached kickoff, Cy felt a deep sense of gratitude. For the volunteers who had given their time. For the parents who had supported the league. For the children who had poured their hearts into every practice and game. And for the community that had embraced the league as its own.

The championship games drew the largest crowds the league had seen all season. Families filled the bleachers, lining the sidelines with folding chairs and blankets. The air buzzed with excitement, and the smell of popcorn and hot chocolate drifted from the concession stand. It felt as though the entire town had gathered to witness the culmination of months of hard work, determination, and community spirit.

Cy moved through the crowd, greeting parents, checking in with coaches, and making sure everything ran smoothly. Despite the chaos, he felt calm.

The first game of the day was the consolation matchup between the third- and fourth-place teams. Though it wasn't the championship, the intensity was unmistakable. Both teams played with heart, pushing themselves to their limits. Parents cheered loudly, and the players responded with determination. Cy watched from the sidelines, feeling a familiar mixture of nerves and excitement. Every tackle, every pass, every touchdown felt like a testament to how far the league had come.

Then came the championship game — Tom's game.

As Tom took the field, Cy felt a level of pride that nearly overwhelmed him. Tom had grown so much over the season — not just as a player, but as a teammate and a young man. He carried himself with confidence, encouraged his teammates, and played with heart. Cy watched him closely, grateful for the chance to witness his son's growth in real time.

The game was close from the start. Both teams fought hard, trading touchdowns and defensive stops. The crowd roared with every big play, and the energy on the field was electric. Tom made several key tackles and even broke free after a short catch for a long run that brought the crowd to its feet. Cy felt his heart race as he watched, knowing how much the moment meant to his son.

In the final minutes, Tom's team trailed by a single touchdown, the score 13–7. The tension was palpable as they lined up for one last drive. Cy held his breath as the quarterback called the play. The ball snapped, the players surged forward, and Tom sprinted downfield. The quarterback launched a pass in his direction. Tom leaped, stretching as far as he could, and caught the ball just before hitting the ground. The crowd erupted.

With seconds left, the team pushed forward again. On third down, they crossed the goal line, tying the game. The extra point would seal the win. The players celebrated wildly, jumping and hugging each other. Parents cheered, some with tears in their eyes. Cy felt a lump in his throat as he watched Tom embrace his teammates, his face glowing with pride.

After the game, Tom ran to him, breathless and beaming.

"Dad! Did you see?"

Cy laughed, pulling him into a hug. "I saw everything. You played your heart out."

Tom grinned, eyes shining. "We did it."

"You sure did," Cy said, feeling a deep, quiet gratitude.

The final championship game brought the season to a close. As the crowd began to disperse, Cy stood quietly for a moment, taking in the scene. The league had created memories that would last a lifetime.

In the days that followed, the excitement in Galesburg lingered like a warm afterglow. Children replayed their favorite moments at school. Parents shared photos and stories at work. Coaches exchanged ideas about how to improve for next season. The league had become a source of pride — a reminder that the town was capable of coming together to create something meaningful. Even those who had been skeptical at first now spoke of the league with admiration.

Cy, however, found himself in a reflective mood. The season had been a whirlwind — full of challenges, triumphs, and moments he knew he would never forget. But now that the games were over and the field was quiet again, he felt a mixture of satisfaction and uncertainty. He had poured so much of himself into the league that he wasn't sure what came next. Still, he knew one thing for certain: the league had changed him, just as it had changed the town.

That evening, Cy sat at the kitchen table with Joanne, discussing the season.

"It's amazing how far this has come," she said. "Do you remember when you first talked about starting a league? It felt like such a long shot."

Cy smiled. "It did. But once things started moving, despite the setbacks, it felt like the town was ready for it."

"They were," Joanne said. "And you were the one who made it happen."

Cy looked down at his hands, feeling a mixture of pride and humility. "I just wanted to give the kids a chance."

"And you did," Joanne replied. "More than that — you gave the town something to believe in."

Later that night, Cy stepped outside to clear his mind. The air was cool, and the stars shone brightly overhead. He thought about the season — the early practices, the long nights of planning, the excitement of game days, and the joy on the children's faces. He realized that the league had become more than a project. It had become a part of him, a reflection of his hopes for the town and for his son.

As he stood there, listening to the quiet of the night, Cy felt a sense of peace. The season had ended, but the journey was far from over. There would be new challenges, new opportunities, and new moments of joy. And he was ready for all of it.

The league had begun as a dream. Now, it was a promise — a promise to the children of Galesburg that they would always have a place to grow, to learn, and to believe in themselves.

WINTER'S QUIET WORK

As November settled over Galesburg, the chill in the air signaled the end of the season and the beginning of a quieter time. The field that had once echoed with laughter, whistles, and the pounding of young feet now sat still beneath a thin layer of frost. Yet even in the silence, it carried the memory of what had taken place — months of growth, determination, and community spirit that had reshaped the town in ways no one could have predicted.

Cy found himself reflecting often during those early winter days. The league had consumed so much of his time and energy that adjusting to the slower pace felt strange. He still had meetings to attend, equipment to store, and plans to consider for the next season — all while keeping up with work and home obligations — but the daily rush of practices and games had faded. In its place was a sense of accomplishment, mixed with a quiet longing for the energy that had filled the fields each week.

One weekend afternoon, while Cy was organizing equipment in the garage, Tom wandered in.

"Dad," he said, "when does football start again?"

Cy smiled. "Not for a while yet. We've got winter to get through first."

Tom nodded, though his disappointment was clear. "I miss it."

"I do too," Cy admitted. "But that's what makes it special. If we played all year, it wouldn't feel the same."

Tom considered this, then asked, "Will the league be even bigger next year?"

Cy paused, thinking about the possibilities. "I think it will. More kids, more teams, maybe even better equipment. We learned a lot this season. Next year will be even stronger."

One evening, as Cy sat at the kitchen table surrounded by papers and folders, Joanne placed a warm cup of coffee beside him.

"You're already planning for next year," she said with a tender smile.

Cy nodded. "There's a lot to think about. If more kids sign up than we expect, we'll need more equipment, more volunteers, maybe even more fields."

Joanne pulled out a chair and sat across from him. "You'll figure it out. You always do."

Cy looked at her, grateful for her steady support. "I just want to make sure the league keeps growing. The kids deserve the best we can give them."

"They do," Joanne agreed. "And you've already given them so much."

Cy paused, reflecting on her words. He thought about the children who had found confidence on the field, the parents who had formed new friendships, and the volunteers who had discovered a renewed sense of purpose. The league had changed lives — his own included.

A few days later, Cy received a letter from a local foundation. They had heard about the league's success and wanted to discuss the possibility of providing a grant for equipment and field improvements. Cy read the letter twice, hardly believing it. This was the kind of support that could transform the league, allowing it to grow in ways he had only imagined.

He shared the news with Joanne and Tom that evening. Tom's eyes widened. "Does that mean we'll get new helmets?"

"Maybe," Cy said with a smile. "It means we'll have a chance to make things even better."

Joanne squeezed his hand. "You see? People believe in what you're doing."

Cy paused in a moment of reflection. The league had begun as a simple idea — a hope born from disappointment — and now it was attracting support from beyond the town. It was becoming something larger, something that could endure.

As the new year approached, Cy continued planning and preparing for the grant interview. On New Year's Eve, as he stood outside watching fireworks burst above the town, he knew there would be many more challenges ahead — funding, logistics, and the inevitable obstacles that came with growth — but he also knew he wasn't facing them alone.

January brought a fresh sense of purpose to Cy's work. The holidays had passed, the decorations were packed away, and the town had settled into the quiet rhythm of winter. But for Cy, the new year marked the beginning of a new chapter for the league. He felt a renewed determination to build on the success of the first season, and now he could potentially have more money than ever to make it happen.

Near the end of January, Cy was scheduled to meet with the local foundation that had notified him of potential grant money. The foundation, All Kids Play, had been raising funds for years to support organizations dedicated to helping children participate in youth sports.

In the days leading up to the interview, Cy prepared diligently. He gathered statistics from the season, compiled testimonials from parents and volunteers, and created a detailed outline of the league's goals. He wanted the foundation to understand not just what the league had accomplished, but what it meant to the community. He wanted them to see the pride in the children's faces, the excitement in the parents' voices, and the sense of unity that had blossomed in Galesburg.

On the morning of the interview, Cy dressed carefully, choosing a clean shirt and his best jacket. He felt nervous, but also confident. He believed in the league, and he believed in the community that had supported it. As he drove to the foundation's office, he rehearsed his talking points, reminding himself of the league's mission and the impact it had already made.

The interview went better than Cy expected. The foundation's representatives listened attentively, asking thoughtful questions about the league's structure, goals, and long-term sustainability. Cy answered each one with honesty and passion, drawing on his experiences from the season. He spoke about the children who had grown in confidence, the parents who had found renewed hope, and the volunteers who had discovered a sense of purpose. By the end of the meeting, he felt a sense of relief. He had done everything he could.

A few days later, Cy received a call from the foundation. They were impressed by his presentation and moved by the league's impact. They wanted to award the grant.

Cy felt a surge of emotion — relief, gratitude, and excitement all at once. He thanked the representative, barely able to contain his joy. This grant would change everything. It would allow the league to purchase new equipment, improve and possibly expand the fields, and reach even more children. It would give the kids of Galesburg opportunities they had never had before.

He shared the news with Joanne and Tom that evening. Tom jumped up and down with excitement. "Does this mean we'll get new jerseys?"

"It means we'll get a lot of things," Cy said with a smile. "Better equipment, better fields, maybe even more teams."

Joanne hugged him tightly. "I'm so proud of you," she said. "You've worked so hard for this."

Cy felt a deep sense of gratitude. The league had begun as a simple idea and now it was growing into something extraordinary. The grant was more than financial support. It was validation — a sign that others believed in the league as much as he did.

As the January snow continued to fall outside, Cy sat at the kitchen table, sketching out plans for the coming season. There was so much to do, so many possibilities to explore. But for the first time, he felt truly prepared. The league had a future — one filled with promise, growth, opportunity, and now sustained funding.

And he was ready to lead it forward.

February arrived with a slow thaw, the kind that hinted at spring even as winter still clung stubbornly to the edges of Galesburg. Cy spent much of the month preparing for the changes ahead. With the grant secured, he now had the resources to make meaningful improvements. He met with equipment suppliers, reviewed catalogs, and compared prices. He wanted to stretch every dollar, ensuring the league received the best possible gear without waste. Helmets, pads, jerseys, practice equipment — everything needed to be upgraded. He approached the task with the same meticulous care he had brought to every aspect of the league.

At home, Tom watched his father with admiration.

"You're really making everything better," he said one evening as Cy reviewed equipment lists at the kitchen table.

"I'm trying," Cy replied. "The kids deserve the best we can give them."

Tom nodded. "I can't wait for next season."

Neither could Cy. The first season had been a success, but he knew the league had the potential to become something even greater — something that would endure for years to come. The grant had opened doors he hadn't even considered before. Now he could think bigger, plan further ahead, and dream without the constant worry of limited resources.

Later that week, Cy attended a meeting he had organized for parents and volunteers to discuss the upcoming season. The room was filled with familiar faces — people who had supported the league from the beginning, as well as new families eager to get involved. The energy felt different this year, fuller somehow, as if the town itself understood that something bigger was taking shape.

Cy outlined the improvements funded by the grant, explained the plans for expanded age groups, and shared his vision for the future. The response was overwhelmingly positive. Parents offered to help with additional fundraising, volunteers signed up for new roles, and several local businesses expressed interest in sponsoring teams. The league was no longer something Cy had to convince people to believe in. It had become something they wanted to be part of.

As the meeting ended, a parent approached Cy with a warm smile.

"You've given this town something to be proud of," she said. "Thank you."

Cy felt a familiar mix of humility and gratitude. "It's the community that made it possible," he said. "I just helped get it started."

As March approached, the first hints of spring began to show. The snow melted slowly, revealing patches of brown grass beneath, and the days grew a little longer, a little brighter. For most people in Galesburg, it was a welcome change. But for Cy, it signaled something more — a shift from planning to action. The new season was drawing closer, and with it came a renewed sense of urgency.

Cy spent much of the month coordinating with suppliers to finalize equipment orders. The grant had opened doors he had only dreamed of, allowing him to purchase high-quality helmets, pads, and jerseys for every team. He wanted the children to feel proud when they stepped onto the field, to know they were part of something special.

One afternoon, after discussing plans with Earl Whitman, Cy met with several contractors to discuss field improvements — reseeded grass, drainage repairs, expanded concessions, new lighting installations. He walked the fields with the project manager, discussing timelines and potential challenges. As he listened to the plans, he felt a surge of excitement. The fields would be transformed — safer, brighter, and better suited for the growing league.

At home, Tom watched the preparations with growing anticipation.

"Do you think we'll get new practice equipment too?" he asked one evening as Cy reviewed invoices.

"We will," Cy said. "Better tackling dummies, new cones, even some training sleds."

Tom's eyes widened. "That's awesome."

Cy smiled, feeling a familiar warmth. Seeing Tom's excitement reminded him why he had started the league in the first place.

Later that week, Cy held a meeting with the volunteer coaches. They gathered in the community center, filling the room with friendly chatter and familiar faces. Cy outlined the improvements for the upcoming season, discussed new safety protocols, and reviewed the expanded age groups. The coaches listened attentively, offering suggestions and asking questions. Their enthusiasm was contagious, and Cy felt grateful for their dedication.

After the meeting, one of the coaches pulled Cy aside.

"You've built something incredible here," he said. "The kids look up to you. The parents trust you. And the town… well, it's different now. Better."

Cy felt a lump in his throat. "It's not just me," he said quietly. "It's everyone who showed up, who believed in the idea."

The coach nodded. "Maybe so. But someone had to start it."

As March drew to a close, Cy stood on the edge of the fields, watching workers prepare the ground for reseeding. The sun was setting, casting a warm glow across the grass. He felt a deep sense of gratitude — for the support of the community, for the dedication of the volunteers, and for the opportunity to build something lasting.

April arrived with a burst of energy that seemed to sweep through the entire town. The fields, once dormant beneath winter's frost, began to show signs of life as the grass turned greener and the days grew warmer. For Cy, the change in season brought a renewed sense of urgency. The new equipment orders were arriving, the field improvements were underway, and the league's second season was fast approaching. There was still much to do, but the excitement building in the community made every task feel worthwhile.

One morning, Cy stood in the garage surrounded by stacks of freshly delivered equipment. Boxes of helmets, shoulder pads, practice jerseys, and training gear filled the space. He opened each box carefully, inspecting the items with a mixture of pride and disbelief. The quality was far better than anything the league had used before. The grant had made it possible, but seeing the equipment in person made the progress feel real.

Tom wandered into the garage, his eyes widening at the sight.

"Whoa," he said. "Is all this for the league?"

"Every bit of it," Cy replied. "We're going to have the best-equipped teams in the county."

Tom picked up a helmet, turning it over in his hands. "These are awesome."

Cy smiled. "I think the kids are going to be pretty excited."

Over the next few days, Cy worked tirelessly to organize the equipment. He labeled boxes, sorted gear by size, and created detailed inventory lists. He wanted everything ready for the coaches' meeting later in the month. The league had grown significantly, and he knew preparation was key to keeping things running smoothly.

Meanwhile, the field improvements were progressing quickly. New lighting poles and a concessions stand were installed, the grass was reseeded, and drainage repairs were nearly complete. Cy visited the fields regularly, checking on the progress and imagining how they would look once the season began. The transformation was remarkable. What had once been worn, uneven ground was becoming a professional-quality space where children could learn and grow.

One afternoon, as Cy walked the fields with the project manager, he felt a deep sense of pride.

"It's really coming together," the manager said. "These fields are going to be some of the best in the region."

Cy nodded. "The kids deserve it."

At home, Joanne noticed the renewed energy in Cy's step.

"You're excited," she said one evening as he reviewed practice schedules.

"I am," Cy admitted. "This season is going to be something special."

"It already is," Joanne replied. "Look at everything you've done."

Cy paused, reflecting on her words. He thought about the long nights of planning, the countless meetings, and the support he had received from the community. The league had grown far beyond his original vision, becoming a source of pride and unity for the town. And now, with the improvements underway, it felt like the league was entering a new chapter.

As April drew to a close, Cy held a meeting with the volunteer coaches to distribute equipment and review the upcoming season. The room buzzed with excitement as the coaches examined the new gear, discussed practice plans, and shared ideas for improving their teams. Cy outlined the changes, emphasized the importance of safety, and encouraged the coaches to continue fostering teamwork and sportsmanship.

As he drove home that evening, Cy felt a deep, settling sense of fulfillment—one that rose slowly, like warmth spreading through his chest. The season was only weeks away now, close enough to touch, and for the first time in months he could see the whole picture clearly. The fields were lined and ready, the equipment sorted and stacked, and the community—his community—was buzzing with anticipation. Parents were talking, kids were counting down the days, and volunteers were stepping forward without being asked.

What had started as a simple idea had grown into something sturdier, something that felt like it belonged to everyone. The league had become more than a program; it had become a symbol of hope, unity, and possibility—a reminder that even in a small town, good things could still blossom and thrive.

As the sun dipped behind the rooftops and the familiar streets of home came into view, Cy felt a quiet certainty settle over him. He had done everything he could to build this foundation. Now it was time to see what would grow from it.

And Cy was ready for the next chapter.

BUILDING THE LADDER

The first week of May brought more than sunshine to Galesburg — it brought clarity. The field was nearly finished, the equipment was sorted, and the coaches were energized. But for Cy, something deeper was stirring. One evening, as he sat at the kitchen table reviewing registration numbers, he noticed a pattern. The sign-ups weren't just increasing — they were spanning a wider age range than ever before. It reminded him of a plan he'd sketched out months earlier, a framework he'd tucked away in the back of his mind.

He flipped through an old notebook and found it — three levels of play: Pee Wee, Pony, and Midget. Pee

Wee would remain the entry point, a place for the youngest boys to learn fundamentals without pressure. Pony would serve the middle age group, introducing more advanced playbooks and positional training. Midget would be the top tier, reserved for the oldest boys, where competition would be tougher and expectations higher. Each level would be determined by age, ensuring every child had a place to play and grow.

But the heart of Cy's vision had always been what came after Pee Wee.

He had imagined the Pony and Midget levels as something more — representative teams selected from the best players in the Pee Wee division. They would act like junior varsity and varsity squads for the Galesburg Youth Football League, competing in an intercity league under the G.G.A.C. banner. And he knew exactly what he wanted to call them.

The Raiders.

It was a name that had lived in Cy's heart since childhood. While Joe had grown up idolizing the Houston Oilers, Cy had been captivated by the swagger, grit, and mystique of the Raiders — the silver and black, the toughness, the attitude that said they belonged on any field, anywhere. As a boy, he'd watched them with wide-eyed admiration, dreaming of playing with that same edge and confidence. Now, he realized he could give that feeling to the kids of Galesburg.

But the name meant more than nostalgia.

It represented the culmination of Cy's original dream: **to build a system that would finally prepare**

Galesburg's boys for high school football. For decades, the town had watched its high school team struggle, year after year, against programs that fed from deep, well-organized youth systems. Cy wanted to change that. He wanted boys entering high school already seasoned — already confident — already understanding the game at a level Galesburg had never seen.

By the time a kid finished as a Raider, Cy thought, he wouldn't just be ready for high school football. He'd be ready to compete.

The next morning, Cy met with league personnel at the community center. He laid out the plan, walking them through each level, explaining how the Pee Wee division would focus on fundamentals, how the Pony and Midget levels would be age-based, and how the Raiders — one Pony team and one Midget team — would be formed from the top players in the Pee Wee ranks.

"We've got the numbers," he said. "We've got the gear. We've got the coaches. And now we've got the funding. This is the year to do it."

The room buzzed with agreement. One volunteer, a retired teacher named Mr. Langford, nodded enthusiastically.

"This gives every kid a place to start," she said. "And something to aim for."

Cy smiled. "Exactly. And by the time they're done as Raiders, they'll be ready for high school. Really ready."

Over the next few days, he worked tirelessly to restructure the league. He divided the registration forms by age group, created separate practice schedules for each level, and began recruiting additional coaches to support the expansion. He met with returning volunteers, explaining the new format and assigning roles based on experience and interest. The response was overwhelming — people wanted to help, wanted to be part of something that felt bigger than just a game.

At home, Tom listened as Cy described the new structure.

"So I'll be in Pee Wee again?" he asked.

"No, you're at Pony level," Cy said. "But you have to keep working hard to get picked for the Raiders."

Tom's eyes widened. "Really?"

Cy nodded. "That's the whole idea. You earn your way up. And by the time you're done, you'll be ready for high school football."

Tom grinned. "I'm gonna practice every day."

Cy laughed. "I believe you."

As the week went on, Cy finalized the rosters, ordered additional equipment for each level, and worked with Joanne to create a flyer explaining the new structure to parents. He wanted everyone to understand the vision — not just the logistics, but the purpose behind it. This wasn't just about football. It was about building a foundation for the future of Galesburg athletics.

One afternoon, Cy stood at the edge of the fields, watching the final lighting tests as dusk settled over Galesburg. The goalposts cast long shadows across the fresh grass, and the new scoreboard blinked to life for the first time. He imagined the Pee Wee teams running drills, the Pony Raiders scrimmaging, and the Midget Raiders preparing for their first out-of-town matchup. He imagined those same boys, years later, stepping onto the high school field with confidence — no longer underdogs, no longer inexperienced, no longer outmatched.

It was all coming together.

Joanne joined him, slipping her arm around his waist.

"You've built something real," she said softly.

Cy nodded, eyes fixed on the field. "And now we're building something lasting. This is how Galesburg finally turns the corner."

By mid-May, the buzz around town was unmistakable. Parents talked about the upcoming season in grocery store aisles, kids tossed footballs in driveways and parks, and volunteers stopped Cy on the street to ask how they could help. The league had always carried a sense of community pride, but this year felt different. Bigger. More purposeful.

Cy felt it most when he walked into the community center for the first official planning session for the new multi-level structure. The room was full — coaches, parents, even a few curious high school players who had heard rumors about "the new system." Cy took his place at the front of the room, his binder thick with notes, schedules, and diagrams.

"Alright," he said, tapping the table lightly. "Let's get started."

He outlined the age-based divisions again — Pee Wee for the youngest boys, Pony for the middle group, and Midget for the oldest. He explained how the Pee Wee division would remain the heart of the league, the place where fundamentals were taught and confidence was built. Then he moved to the part that made his pulse quicken.

"The Pony and Midget Raiders," he said, "will be our representative teams. They'll be chosen from the top players in Pee Wee each year. They'll practice separately, compete in an intercity league, and represent the G.G.A.C."

He had already spoken with a couple of leagues within an hour's drive, both of which showed strong interest in bringing the Raiders aboard — and the East Valley League had all but guaranteed it. That was enough for Cy to keep his dream moving forward at full speed.

A murmur of excitement rippled through the room.

Cy continued, "By the time a kid finishes as a Raider, he'll have years of structured training, real competition experience, and a deep understanding of the game. When he gets to high school, he won't be starting from scratch. He'll be ready."

A coach in the back nodded. "This is how the big programs do it."

Cy smiled. "Exactly. And it's how Galesburg is going to do it from now on."

The meeting stretched late into the evening as coaches volunteered for roles, parents offered to help with transportation and fundraising, and committee members discussed logistics for the Raiders' intercity schedule. Cy left the building feeling lighter than he had in months. The dream he'd carried since the very beginning — giving Galesburg a real football foundation — was finally taking shape.

The next week, Cy held the first evaluation session for the Pee Wee division. Boys from all over town showed up, bundled in mismatched athletic gear, some nervous, some bursting with excitement. Cy watched them run drills, throw passes, and learn basic formations. He saw raw talent, determination, and the kind of enthusiasm that reminded him why he'd started all this.

As he observed, he couldn't help imagining the future. Some of these boys would one day wear the dark blue and white of the Raiders. He chose those colors instead of the traditional Raider silver and black to honor the Penn State Nittany Lions; for many blue-collar Pennsylvanians, Penn State football isn't just a team — it's a cultural anchor, a point of pride, and a reflection of who they are. He wanted the same for his Raiders.

He imagined how some of his players would go on to high school ready to compete at a level Galesburg hadn't seen in decades. And some — maybe a few — might even develop enough to represent Galesburg at Penn State. More likely, many would simply grow into confident young men because of the lessons they learned here.

That, Cy thought, was the real victory.

A few days later, Cy met with the high school football coach, a man who had grown accustomed to rebuilding seasons and lopsided losses. When Cy explained the new structure, the coach leaned back in his chair, eyebrows raised.

"You're telling me," he said slowly, "that in a few years, I'll be getting freshmen who already know how to read a defense?"

Cy nodded. "And block properly. And tackle safely. And run real plays. And handle pressure."

The coach let out a low whistle. "This could change everything."

"That's the plan," Cy said.

For the first time in a long time, the high school coach looked hopeful.

As May turned to June, the Raiders concept began to feel real. Cy ordered new jerseys for both the Pony and Midget teams — simple, bold, unmistakably inspired by Penn State. When the boxes arrived, he opened one and held a jersey in his hands. The fabric was crisp, the colors striking.

Joanne walked into the garage and smiled. "They look professional."

"They are," Cy said quietly. "These kids are going to feel like they're part of something big."

He imagined the first time the Raiders would take the field — how the town would react, how the boys would stand a little taller, how opposing teams would see Galesburg not as an afterthought, but as a program on the rise.

It was all coming full circle.

The dream he'd had on that long drive months ago — the dream of building a system that would finally give Galesburg a fighting chance — was no longer just an idea. It was happening. Piece by piece, practice by practice, season by season.

And Cy knew, deep down, that years from now, when the first wave of Raiders stepped onto the high school field, seasoned and confident, the town would remember this moment. The moment everything began to change.

Cy locked up the garage, the new jerseys still folded neatly on the table. The sun was setting, casting a warm glow across the land. He stood there for a long moment, hands in his pockets, breathing in the quiet evening air.

For the first time, he didn't just hope Galesburg could compete.

He believed it.

THE MAKING OF A RAIDER

The first Saturday of June dawned warm and bright, the kind of early summer morning that made Galesburg feel alive again. Dew clung to the grass, the air carried a faint sweetness, and the newly improved field looked almost unreal in the soft light. Today wasn't just another league event. Today was the beginning of something Cy had dreamed about since the very first spark of the league.

It was Raiders Tryout Day.

By eight o'clock, families were already gathering along the sidelines. Boys from every corner of town jogged onto the field, some bouncing with excitement, others quiet and focused. They wore mismatched shirts and shorts, but each one carried the same hope — to earn a spot on the Pony or Midget Raiders, the teams that would represent Galesburg in the intercity league.

Cy stood near midfield, clipboard in hand, watching the boys warm up. He felt a familiar flutter in his chest — not nerves, exactly, but something close. Anticipation. Pride. The sense that this was a turning point.

Coach Stosh walked up beside him, arms crossed, eyes scanning the field. Cy had recruited him to coach the Pony Raiders for the inaugural season.

"Look at this turnout," Stosh said. "You'd think we were running a college camp."

Cy grinned. "Feels like the start of something big."

"It is," Stosh replied.

Cy didn't answer. He just watched the boys stretching, laughing, shaking out their arms. He saw Tom among them, helmet tucked under his arm, eyes bright with determination. And he saw older boys too — kids who had played last season and had grown an inch or two since then, kids who were starting to look like real football players.

The whistle blew, and tryouts began.

The coaches ran the boys through a series of drills — footwork ladders, passing accuracy, tackling form on the new padded sleds, sprint times, agility tests. Cy moved from station to station, taking notes, watching closely. He wasn't looking for perfection. He was looking for potential. For heart. For the spark that could be shaped into something more.

At the tackling station, he watched a boy named Marcus — small for his age, but fearless — drive into the sled with perfect form.

"That kid's got something," Stosh muttered.

Cy nodded.

"Raider material," Stosh finished.

At the passing station, an older boy named Dan launched a tight spiral that cut through the air like a dart. The coaches exchanged glances.

"Quarterback for the Midget Raiders," one whispered.

Cy felt a wave of pride. These weren't just kids running around anymore. They were players. Developing. Growing. Becoming.

This was the system working.

By midday, the sun was high and the boys were exhausted, but the energy on the field never dipped. Parents watched anxiously from the sidelines, whispering about who looked fast, who looked strong, who might make the cut. The dark blue and white Raiders banners Joanne had helped design fluttered in the breeze, giving the field a sense of ceremony.

During a break, Tom jogged over to Cy, cheeks flushed, breathing hard.

"How am I doing?" he asked.

Cy smiled. "You're working. That's what matters."

Tom nodded, wiping sweat from his forehead. "I really want this."

"I know," Cy said. "And no matter what happens today, you keep working. Raiders or not, this is just the beginning."

Tom nodded again, more serious this time, then ran back to join the others.

Cy watched him go, feeling a mix of pride and something deeper — the realization that this system wasn't just shaping players. It was shaping boys into young men.

In the afternoon, the coaches gathered under the shade of the concession stand to compare notes. Clipboards were stacked, names circled, comments scribbled in margins. The discussions were intense but respectful — every coach understood the weight of the decisions.

"These kids are going to represent Galesburg," Stosh said. "We pick the ones who are ready to work, ready to learn, ready to compete."

Cy nodded. "And ready to grow."

When the lists were finalized, Cy held the papers in his hands for a long moment. The names weren't just names. They were the first generation of Raiders — the first boys who would climb the ladder he had built, the first who would one day step onto the high school field already seasoned, already confident, already ready.

This was the beginning of the dream coming full circle.

As the sun dipped low, families gathered around the field for the announcement. The boys stood shoulder to shoulder, some bouncing nervously, others staring straight ahead. Cy stepped forward, the lists folded in his hand.

He took a breath.

"Today," he began, "you all made Galesburg proud. You worked hard. You pushed yourselves. You showed heart. And that's what this league is all about."

He paused, letting the moment settle.

"But the Raiders… the Raiders are something special. They're the teams that will represent our town. They're the teams that will compete in the intercity league. And one day, they'll be the players who walk into Galesburg High School ready to win."

A ripple of excitement moved through the crowd.

Cy unfolded the list.

"And now," he said, "let's meet the first Raiders."

That evening, long after the families had gone home and the field had grown quiet again, Cy stood alone near the fifty-yard line. The sky was streaked with orange and purple, and the new lights hummed softly overhead.

He thought about the boys who had made the team. He thought about the ones who hadn't — and how they would keep working. He thought about the future, about the seasons to come, about the day when the first wave of Raiders would step onto the high school field and change everything.

For the first time, the dream didn't feel distant. It felt inevitable.

The first official Raiders practice kicked off on a warm Saturday morning in mid-July. The sun was already high, the grass still damp, and the boys arrived sporadically. Some looked ready. Some looked terrified. All of them looked like they understood something new was happening in Galesburg.

Cy stood at midfield, clipboard tucked under his arm, watching the groups form. This was the moment he'd been working toward for months. But as the boys spread out and the whistles started, he felt a pressure he hadn't anticipated. Not from parents or the committee — this was internal. He'd raised the bar. Now he had to live up to it.

A sharp whistle cut through the chatter.

"Pony Raiders over here!" Stosh barked, waving his arm like he was directing traffic on a busy highway.

"Midget Raiders on the far side!" Coach Dwyer shouted. He had coached Tom's championship Pee Wee team, and Cy knew talent when he saw it. That's why he'd recruited Dwyer to take charge of the Midget Raiders.

The boys scrambled. Stosh — broad-shouldered, gravel-voiced, and already sweating through his cap — looked perfectly at home. He'd coached Pee Wee kids last year, but this was different. This time he'd been handed a group expected to represent Galesburg beyond its borders.

Cy scanned the Pony group and spotted Tom — helmet tucked under his arm, trying to look calm but failing miserably. Tom had made the Pony Raiders after all. Cy had kept the evaluations blind, just numbers and notes. When Tom's number landed in the top group, Cy felt a quiet surge of pride. The kid had earned it.

"Alright, boys," Stosh growled, pacing in front of them. "You're Raiders now. That means you work harder than you ever have. You listen. You hustle. And you don't quit. Not here."

The boys nodded, some swallowing hard.

Practice opened with conditioning — sprints, backpedals, agility ladders. The Midget group handled it well. The Pony boys... not so much. A few lagged behind. One sat down clutching his side. Another muttered that Pee Wee had never been this tough.

"That's the point," Stosh said under his breath as he passed Cy. "They'll get there."

Cy hoped he was right.

During a water break, Cy stepped away from the field and headed toward the small equipment shed where a representative from the East Valley Intercity League was waiting for him. The man had driven in that morning from East Valley — a tall, no-nonsense type in a league windbreaker who carried a folder under his arm and the air of someone who'd spent half his life around football fields. They sat at a metal table in the cramped coaches' room going over paperwork and reviewing the league's expectations. After a few final questions and a long, considering look, the representative closed the folder, tapped it once with his knuckles, and told Cy what he'd been hoping to hear: the G.G.A.C. Raiders — both

Ponies and Midgets — had been accepted into the East Valley Intercity League, one of the toughest youth circuits in the region.

East Valley wasn't just another town. It was a blue-collar steel community where toughness wasn't a slogan — it was a way of life. Their youth teams had reputations built on grit, discipline, and a brand of football that felt closer to high school than middle school. The league included programs from East Valley, Iron Hill, Millstone, and a handful of other factory towns where Friday nights were sacred and football was a badge of pride.

Getting in hadn't been easy. Cy had spent weeks over the winter driving to meetings, mailing rosters, and sending packets of facility photos and program outlines. He'd pitched the Raiders as a rising program with structure, community backing, and a clear developmental path. The league board had been skeptical at first — Galesburg wasn't known for producing powerhouse teams — but Cy's persistence wore them down. Their initial doubts slowly shifted toward curiosity, then respect, and finally acceptance.

Now it was official. Now the Raiders were in. Ten regular-season games. Five at home. Five on the road. And every opponent would be tough.

As the representative pulled out of the parking lot, Cy exhaled slowly. Excitement mixed with nerves. This was a big step — maybe bigger than he'd realized. He'd started the Raiders with the assumption they would have a league to play in. It had always felt implied, but only now was it real. Relief left him like dust shaken from an old coat.

He returned to the field just in time to see Tom stumble during a footwork drill. The boy popped up quickly, but Cy caught the frustration in his eyes.

Stosh blew his whistle. "Tom! Reset! Don't think — just move!"

Tom nodded and ran the drill again, cleaner this time.

As practice wore on, the challenges became clearer. Some boys struggled with the pace. Others looked overwhelmed by the more advanced playbook. A few parents lingered at the fence, whispering concerns about the intensity.

Cy felt every bit of it.

But he also saw flashes of what the Raiders could become. A perfect route from a quiet kid who barely spoke. A clean tackle from a boy who'd been timid in Pee Wee. Tom finishing a drill with grit after stumbling early.

When practice finally ended, the boys dragged themselves off the field — sweaty, exhausted, but smiling.

Tom jogged over, cheeks flushed. "Dad… that was awesome."

Cy laughed, the tension easing. "Tougher than Pee Wee?"

"Way tougher," Tom said proudly. "But I can do it."

Cy put a hand on his shoulder. "Yes, you can."

As the field emptied and the sun dipped lower, Cy stood alone for a moment, taking it all in. The Raiders were real. The East Valley league was real. The expectations were real.

And so were the challenges.

But for the first time that day, he felt something stronger than pressure.

He felt belief.

STEEL IN THE GRASS

The Raiders' first scrimmage came fast. Just five weeks into practice, the East Valley Intercity League sent word: Millstone was available for a preseason matchup. Cy didn't hesitate. He wanted to see what his boys could do.

The Saturday afternoon of the scrimmage arrived with a breeze and a crowd. The field was freshly lined, the bleachers full, and the concession stand humming. The same banner hung on the fence behind the home sideline — **GO RAIDERS!** — its corners flapping like it had something to prove.

Stosh stood at the center of the Pony Raiders huddle, arms crossed, voice low and steady. "This ain't

Pee Wee anymore," he said. "You're gonna get hit. You're gonna get pushed. You don't back down. You hit back."

The boys nodded, some more than others.

Millstone's team arrived quiet and focused. They didn't smile. They didn't wave. They walked onto the field like they'd done it a hundred times before.

Cy felt the difference immediately.

The Pony Raiders took the field first. Tom lined up at slot receiver, helmet on, mouthguard tucked behind his ear. He looked ready. Nervous, but ready.

The first snap was clean. The quarterback rolled right and fired a short pass. Tom caught it, turned upfield — and was flattened by a Millstone linebacker.

The crowd gasped.

Cy winced.

Tom popped up, shook his head, and jogged back to the huddle.

Stosh clapped once. "Good. Now do it again."

The next series showed promise — a few short gains, a solid block, a tackle that drew cheers. But Millstone's boys were sharper, faster, more confident. They'd been playing at this level for years. The Raiders were still learning what it meant to compete outside Galesburg.

By the end of the half, the scoreboard leaned heavily toward Millstone. But the Pony Raiders hadn't folded. They'd taken hits, made adjustments, and kept fighting.

Cy felt proud. Not satisfied — but proud. He offered the team encouragement and some orange slices for added energy.

As the second half began, Cy stood near the fence, watching the boys regroup. He saw bruises, grass stains, and tired eyes. But he also saw resolve.

Tom jogged past, breathing hard. "They're good," he said. "Really good."

Cy nodded. "So are you."

Tom smiled. "We'll get there."

Cy looked out at the field. The Raiders were behind. But they were in it. They were learning. They were growing.

And they were tougher than he'd expected.

As the final whistle blew and the teams shook hands, Cy felt something shift. The Raiders hadn't won. But they'd shown up. They'd taken hits. They'd stood their ground.

East Valley football was real. Steel-town tough. But Galesburg had steel in its grass too.

Then came the Midget Raiders.

They looked bigger. Stronger. More polished. But the moment the game began, it was clear Millstone's Midget squad was on another level.

The first drive ended in a sack. The second in a fumble. The third in a pick-six that drew groans from the home crowd.

Cy watched from the sideline, arms crossed, jaw tight.

The hits were harder. The gaps wider. The speed difference undeniable.

By the fourth quarter, the Raiders were down by four touchdowns. The boys looked dazed. The coaches shouted, adjusted, encouraged — but the momentum never shifted.

Cy felt it in his chest. That creeping doubt.

Had he pushed too fast? Too far?

The intercity league was tougher than he'd imagined. East Valley football wasn't just organized — it was hardened. These towns raised boys who grew up around steel mills and long shifts. Football wasn't just a game. It was identity.

As the final whistle blew and the teams shook hands, Cy stood quietly near the fence. The Raiders hadn't quit. But they'd been outmatched.

He looked out at the field — grass torn, helmets scuffed, boys limping toward the sideline.

They had heart. No question.

But heart alone wouldn't be enough.

The field was empty the next morning, dew still clinging to the grass, the scoreboard dark. Cy unlocked the equipment shed and carried a folding table into the small meeting room the coaches used on Sundays. One by one, they arrived — Stosh first, coffee in hand, then Coach Dwyer from the Midget squad, and finally the assistants who had spent the scrimmage pacing the sidelines with clipboards and worried expressions.

No one spoke at first. They all knew what the film would show.

Cy set the projector, dimmed the lights, and hit play.

The Pony Raiders appeared first — Tom catching that early pass, the Millstone linebacker flattening him, the boys scrambling to adjust to the speed and physicality.

Stosh leaned forward, elbows on his knees. "They weren't scared," he said. "That's something. They got hit, but they didn't fold."

Cy nodded. "Footwork needs work. Angles too. And conditioning."

"Conditioning most of all," Stosh said. "They're not used to playing boys who've been in pads since they were six."

They watched a few more plays — some promising, some painful. A couple of good blocks. A clean tackle. A blown assignment that led to a long run.

"They can get there," Stosh said finally. "But we've got to toughen them up. And fast."

Cy heard the confidence in his voice. It helped. A little.

Then the Midget footage began.

The room grew quiet.

Millstone's Midget squad looked like a different species — bigger, faster, more disciplined. The Raiders' first drive ended in a sack. The second in a fumble. The third in a pick-six that still made Cy's stomach tighten.

Coach Dwyer rubbed his forehead. "We weren't ready for that speed," he said. "They were reading us like a book."

Cy rewound a play where the Raiders' defensive line was pushed back three yards before the running back even touched the ball.

"That's strength," Dwyer said. "Pure strength. We don't have it yet."

The assistants murmured in agreement.

Another clip showed a Millstone receiver blowing past the secondary untouched.

"That's discipline," Cy said quietly. "They don't take false steps. They don't guess. They react."

The room stayed silent for a long moment.

Cy paused the film and turned on the lights. The coaches blinked, adjusting.

"Alright," he said. "We know what we're up against. East Valley football is different. It's tougher. Faster. More physical. We can't pretend otherwise."

Stosh crossed his arms. "So we don't pretend. We fix it."

Coach Dwyer nodded. "We need to rebuild our conditioning plan. More sprints. More strength work. And we simplify the playbook. They're thinking too much."

"Agreed," Cy said. "And tackling. We need to teach them how to finish tackles, not just make contact."

One of the assistants spoke up. "And blocking. Our boys aren't firing off the line. They're waiting."

Cy wrote it all down — conditioning, strength, tackling, blocking, simplified schemes.

The list felt long.

Too long.

When the meeting ended and the coaches filed out, Cy stayed behind. He stared at the empty chairs, the silent projector, the notes scattered across the table.

He'd known the East Valley league would be tough. But he hadn't expected the gap to feel this wide.

For the first time since the Raiders were formed, doubt crept in — not a wave, but a quiet, persistent whisper.

Had he pushed too fast? Too far? Was Galesburg ready for this level of football? Were the boys?

He closed the notebook and exhaled slowly.

Ready or not, the first official game was coming. And the Raiders would have to meet it head-on.

Cy stood, turned off the lights, and stepped out into the sun. The field stretched before him — quiet now, but full of possibility.

They had work to do.

And it started tomorrow.

FIRST BLOOD

Monday late afternoon arrived with no fanfare. No music. No pep talks. Just a whistle and a new tempo.

Practice started at 6:00 p.m. sharp. By 6:03, the boys were already sweating.

Stosh stood at the edge of the field, stopwatch in hand, barking out intervals like a drill sergeant. "Sprints! Thirty seconds! Go!"

The Pony Raiders took off, legs pumping, faces tight with effort. No one jogged. No one coasted. The message had been clear: the old way was gone.

Cy watched from the sideline, clipboard in hand, tracking reps and heart rates. The Midget squad was on the far end of the field, running cone drills under Coach Dwyer's watchful eye. Assistants moved between groups, correcting stances, adjusting footwork, pushing tempo.

Everything was faster now.

Everything was sharper.

The playbooks had been trimmed. No more layered schemes or exotic formations. Just fundamentals — blocking, tackling, pursuit angles, ball security. The coaches drilled the same concepts over and over until the boys could execute them without thinking.

"Eyes up!" Dwyer shouted. "Don't guess — read!"

"Drive through the hips!" Stosh barked. "Finish the tackle!"

The boys responded. Slowly at first. Then with growing confidence.

Tom ran a route with crisp footwork and caught a pass in stride. A lineman who'd struggled in the scrimmage pancaked his defender in a blocking drill. A cornerback who'd been burned by Millstone's speed stayed step-for-step with his man through a full rep.

Cy saw it happening.

The shift.

But progress came with pain.

One boy threw up after sprints. Another limped off with a twisted ankle. A few sat on the bench, heads down, trying to catch their breath.

Cy walked past them, offering water and quiet encouragement. He didn't sugarcoat it. "This is what it takes," he said. "If you want to compete in East Valley, this is the price."

Some nodded.

Some just stared.

He understood. The scrimmage had exposed the gap. Now they were trying to close it. But closing it meant breaking old habits, pushing past comfort, and learning to fight through fatigue.

It wasn't glamorous.

It was work.

As the sun dipped low and the final whistle blew, the boys dragged themselves off the field — sore, tired, but sharper than they'd been a week ago.

Cy gathered the coaches near the shed.

"They're responding," he said. "But we've got to keep pressing. First game's in five days."

Dwyer nodded. "We'll be ready."

Stosh cracked his neck. "They'll be tougher. That's what matters."

Cy looked out at the field, now quiet and golden in the fading light. The Raiders were changing. Not just in skill, but in mindset.

They weren't ready yet.

But they were getting there.

And for the first time since Millstone, Cy believed they might belong. He needed that belief.

The Raiders' first official league game was set for a cool Saturday afternoon in early September. The buses rolled in from Iron Hill, another East Valley town with a reputation for hard-nosed football and steel in its veins. Their boys stepped off in matching gear, quiet and focused, confident they had already won the game.

Cy stood near the gate, watching them file in. He didn't say much. Just nodded to the league rep, checked the roster sheets, and walked back toward the field.

The Raiders were already warming up — faster, sharper, more focused than they'd ever been. The last two weeks had changed them. Practices were harder. Expectations were higher. And the boys had started to carry themselves differently.

But Cy knew confidence only went so far.

Stosh led the Pony squad onto the field first. Tom jogged beside him, helmet on, eyes forward. The crowd was bigger than expected — parents, neighbors, even a few curious faces from the high school.

The opening kickoff was clean. The Raiders recovered it and started their drive at the thirty-five.

First play: a short run up the middle. Two yards.

Second play: a swing pass to Tom. He caught it, turned upfield, and broke a tackle before being pushed out of bounds.

Third play: a miscommunication. The quarterback rolled left, the receiver broke right. Incomplete.

Fourth down.

Stosh didn't hesitate. "Punt team!"

The boys jogged off, heads high. No panic. No collapse.

Iron Hill's offense was fast, but the Raiders held. A tackle for loss. A pass breakup. A third-down stop that drew cheers from the sideline.

Cy felt something stir in his chest.

They were competing.

The rest of the half was a grind — three-and-outs, punts, hard tackles. The Raiders gave up a touchdown late, but they didn't fold. They hit back. They adjusted. They stayed in it.

Halftime score: Iron Hill 7, Raiders 3.

Respectable.

Earned.

The first half had been a grind, but the Raiders hung tough, and Stosh's halftime talk lit a spark.

Early in the third quarter, the Raiders recovered a fumble near midfield. Two plays later, Tom caught a quick slant, broke a tackle, and sprinted down the sideline before being pushed out at the ten. The crowd roared. Three plays after that, the Raiders punched it in.

Raiders 10, Iron Hill 7.

The sideline erupted. Parents pounded the fence. Stosh pumped his fist once — his version of a victory dance.

And the boys believed.

They carried that belief deep into the fourth quarter. The defense held strong. The offense chewed clock. Every minute that ticked away felt like a miracle.

With just under three minutes left, the Raiders still led 10–7.

Cy could feel the tension in the air. The boys could too.

Iron Hill stacked the box, daring the Raiders to throw. Stosh called a simple sweep — safe, familiar, something they'd run a hundred times.

But nerves change everything.

The snap was a little high. The quarterback bobbled it. The timing was off. The running back hesitated. A defender shot through untouched.

The ball popped loose.

Iron Hill scooped it up and ran it back thirty yards before being tackled.

Two plays later, Iron Hill scored.

Iron Hill 14, Raiders 10.

The Raiders got the ball back with less than a minute left, but the panic had set in. A false start. A dropped pass. A sack. And then the clock ran out.

The boys stood there, stunned, helmets hanging at their sides.

They had been *this close*.

The scoreboard said loss. But the crowd didn't see a losing team. They saw a group of boys who had gone toe-to-toe with an East Valley powerhouse and nearly shocked the entire league. They saw heart, grit, and flashes of something rare.

Stosh gathered the boys at midfield. His voice was low but steady. "You didn't lose today," he said. "You learned. And next year, when you're Midgets… you're gonna give those big boys hell."

The parents cheered. Some even wiped away tears. They knew what they had just witnessed.

Cy watched Tom walk off the field — tired, disappointed, but standing tall. The whole Pony squad carried themselves that way. They weren't broken.

They were becoming something.

Something real.

Something dangerous.

And Cy knew, deep down, that when these boys moved up next season, the Midget league wouldn't know what hit them.

Then came the Midget game.

Coach Dwyer had spent the week reshaping the playbook, drilling fundamentals, pushing tempo. The boys looked ready. But Iron Hill's Midget squad was something else — bigger, faster, meaner.

The first drive ended in a sack.

The second in a punt.

The third in a pick-six.

Cy watched from the sideline, arms crossed, concerned.

By the end of the first quarter, it was 21–0.

The Raiders looked stunned. The crowd quieted. Dwyer paced the sideline, shouting adjustments, but the momentum never shifted.

Iron Hill's boys didn't just play football. They imposed it.

By the fourth quarter, the score was 35–0.

Cy felt the doubt return. Not loud. Not dramatic. Just a quiet whisper in the back of his mind.

Had they come far enough? Were they truly ready for this league?

He looked out at the field — grass torn, helmets scuffed, boys limping back to the sideline.

They hadn't quit.

But they'd certainly been outclassed.

When the final whistle blew, the teams shook hands. The Iron Hill coaches nodded respectfully. No gloating. Just business.

Cy gathered the boys near the shed. He didn't give a speech. Just looked them in the eyes.

"You showed heart," he said. "But heart's not enough. Not here. Not in this league."

They nodded, quiet and tired. Disappointed — but not defeated.

Cy saw it.

They were still in this.

Still building.

Still climbing.

But the mountain was taller than they'd thought.

Sunday morning came quiet and gray, the kind of early fall stillness that made the whole town feel like it was catching its breath. Cy opened the equipment shed and stepped inside, the familiar smell of cut grass and old pads hanging in the air. He set a stack of notebooks on the table, powered up the projector, and waited.

Stosh arrived first, coffee in hand, jaw set but eyes still burning with the pride of yesterday's near miracle.

Coach Dwyer followed, shoulders heavy from the Midget loss but ready to face it. The assistants trickled in behind them, some carrying clipboards, others just carrying the weight of what they'd seen.

No one spoke at first.

Cy dimmed the lights and hit play.

The screen lit up with the second half of the Pony game — Tom's slant route, the broken tackle, the sideline roar. The fumble recovery. The touchdown. The defensive stand that had the crowd on its feet.

Stosh leaned forward, elbows on his knees. "Look at 'em," he said quietly. "They weren't supposed to hang with Iron Hill. But they didn't just hang — they pushed 'em."

Cy nodded. "They played like they belonged."

They watched the final minutes — the nerves, the panic, the fumbled sweep that changed everything. The boys' faces afterward, stunned but proud.

"That mistake?" Stosh said. "That's youth. That's nerves. That's not who they are — that's who they are *right now.*"

The assistants murmured in agreement.

Cy paused the film on a frame of the boys walking off the field — tired, disappointed, but standing tall.

"They're special," he said. "Next year, when they're Midgets… they're going to shake this league."

Stosh cracked a rare smile. "They're gonna do more than shake it."

Then Cy switched to the Midget footage.

The room fell silent.

Iron Hill's size and speed were undeniable. The Raiders' mistakes were glaring. Missed blocks. Missed tackles. Confusion in the secondary. A fumble that never should've happened. A pick-six that broke their momentum before they ever had any.

Coach Dwyer rubbed his forehead. "We weren't ready," he said. "Not for that level. Not yet."

Cy didn't sugarcoat it. "They're bigger. Stronger. More disciplined. They've been playing this brand of football for years."

One assistant pointed at the screen. "Look at their line. They fire off like a single unit. Our boys… they're still thinking."

"Thinking gets you beat," Dwyer said. "Reacting wins games."

They watched another series — Iron Hill's running back bursting through a gap untouched.

"That's strength," Cy said. "And conditioning. And confidence."

The room stayed quiet for a long moment.

Cy turned off the projector and flipped on the lights. The coaches blinked, adjusting again.

"Alright," he said. "We know where we stand. The Ponies showed us what's possible. The Midgets showed us what's required."

Stosh nodded. "We build from the bottom up. But those Pony boys — they're the future."

Dwyer exhaled. "And we rebuild the Midgets. Strip it down. Fundamentals. Strength. Conditioning. Even less fancy stuff."

Cy wrote it all down — a revised blueprint forming in his mind.

"We're not backing out of this league," he said. "We're not lowering the bar. We're raising our boys to meet it."

The coaches nodded, some with renewed fire, others with quiet determination.

When the meeting ended, the coaches filed out one by one. Cy stayed behind, reflecting again.

The Ponies had shown heart — real heart. Enough to scare a steel-town powerhouse. Enough to make the crowd believe. Enough to make Cy believe.

The Midgets had shown the truth — the gap was real, and it was wide.

But gaps could be closed.

Programs could grow.

And next year, when those Pony boys moved up… everything would change.

Cy stepped outside into the cool September air. The field stretched before him, quiet and full of promise.

They had work to do.

And now, they had a direction.

FIRST TASTE OF VICTORY

The third week of the season arrived with a mix of nerves and stubborn determination. Week One had shown promise for the Ponies and harsh reality for the Midgets. Week Two had been worse — both teams outclassed, outmuscled, and outscored. The Ponies had fought hard but still fell short, and the Midgets… well, East Valley football didn't give sympathy points.

But Week Three brought something different.
A road trip.

The Raiders were scheduled to play the Millstone Mustangs — the same teams that had handed both the Pony and Midget squads decisive losses in the preseason scrimmage. The games were set for Saturday morning, and for the first time, the boys would ride together on a chartered bus. After two straight losses, the idea of traveling as a real team — on a real bus — felt like a spark they desperately needed.

Cy stood by the curb as the boys climbed aboard, their duffel bags bouncing against their legs, helmets clutched tight. The bus wasn't new, but to the kids it might as well have been a luxury liner. Wide seats. Overhead racks. Air-conditioning that actually worked.

Tom slid into a window seat near the front, watching the town drift by as the bus pulled away. He didn't talk much. He didn't need to. The ride itself was magic.

Stosh walked the aisle, handing out water bottles and tapping helmets. "This ain't a field trip," he said. "It's a business trip. But you can enjoy the ride."

The boys grinned anyway.

Millstone's stadium rose out of the ground like something from a different world. Bleachers on both sides. A scoreboard with bright red digits. Painted end zones. A press box with tinted windows. Even a concession stand that smelled like popcorn and grilled onions.

The Raiders stepped off the bus and froze.

"Holy crap," one whispered.

Cy let them stare for a moment. Then he clapped his hands sharply.

"Warm up. You earned this field. Now show it."

They jogged out, pads clacking, voices rising, the awe slowly turning into energy.

The Mustangs were bigger. Faster. More polished than they remembered — or at least it seemed so. But the Raiders had something new: resolve born from two straight losses.

The Pony game kicked off first.

First quarter: They recovered a fumble after punching the ball loose and scored. **Second quarter:** Tom caught a swing pass, cut inside, then outside, and dove for the pylon. Touchdown.

Halftime score: **Raiders 12, Mustangs 6.**

Cy didn't smile. But he felt something shifting.

Third quarter: A long drive stalled at the ten. Fourth down. Stosh called timeout.

He knelt in the huddle. "You want this? Then take it."

They did.

Tom caught a quick down-and-out to the left, planted, cut back inside, and stretched the ball over the goal line.

Fourth quarter: The Mustangs scored again, tightening the gap. But the Raiders held. Two tackles for loss. A pass breakup. A final kneel-down.

Final score: Raiders 18, Mustangs 12.

Their first win.

The Midget Raiders' Week Three matchup was supposed to steady them after two bruising losses. Instead, it became another long afternoon that exposed just how far behind they still were. From the opening kickoff, Millstone pushed them around — bigger linemen collapsing the pocket, faster backs slipping through arm tackles, and a quarterback who seemed to complete every throw.

By halftime, the Raiders trailed by four touchdowns. The sideline felt heavy, quiet, unsure.

The second half didn't offer much relief. A few bright moments — a hard tackle by Luis, a near interception by Billy, a rare first down — sparked brief flickers of hope, but Millstone smothered each one. When the final whistle blew, the scoreboard read **42–0**, and the Midgets trudged to the handshake line with shoulders slumped and eyes down.

The coaches didn't scold them. They didn't need to. The boys already knew the truth: they weren't ready yet. But beneath the disappointment, Cy sensed something else beginning to form — not confidence, not yet, but a kind of stubborn resolve. Losses like this either break a team or harden it. He just had to make sure it was the latter.

The bus — at least the portion holding the Pony team — was a rolling thunderstorm of joy. Boys sang, shouted, replayed every moment. Helmets clattered. Shoulder pads squeaked. Someone started a chant that lasted half the ride.

Cy sat near the back, watching it all. He didn't join in. He didn't need to. He just let the sound wash over him.

Two straight losses had tested them. This win meant more because of it.

Later, Cy looked at Tom asleep against the window, mouth slightly open, helmet resting in his lap.

They were still kids.

But they were becoming Raiders.

The Monday after the road-trip win carried a different energy the moment Cy stepped onto Whitman Field. The air wasn't lighter — three straight Midget losses made sure of that — but something underneath had shifted. The Ponies' breakthrough had cracked open a door the whole program needed. It didn't erase the bruises or the scoreboard from the Midgets' 42–0 beating, but it reminded everyone that progress wasn't a fantasy.

It was possible.

The Midgets drifted in slowly, helmets dangling from fingertips, cleats dragging through the grass. They weren't sulking so much as carrying a weight they didn't know how to set down. Cy watched them carefully — the slumped shoulders, the quiet greetings, the way none of them looked toward the scoreboard even though it was blank.

Dwyer blew his whistle once, sharp and commanding.

"Stretch line! Let's move."

The boys obeyed, but without urgency. Cy stepped forward.

"Listen up," he said, voice steady. "Saturday was rough. No one's pretending otherwise. But that game doesn't get to define you unless you let it."

A few heads lifted.

"You got beat by a team that's been together for years. You've been together for only weeks. That's not failure — that's math."

A couple of the boys cracked the smallest smiles.

Cy nodded. "What matters now is what you do next. You want to get better? Then today is where it starts."

He clapped once, loud and sharp. "Warm-up jog. Two laps. Go."

The boys took off, and for the first time since Saturday, they didn't look defeated — they looked determined.

That evening, Cy, Stosh, and Dwyer sat in the cramped equipment shed behind Whitman Field, the portable projector humming against the wall. They watched the Midgets' game again — slowly, painfully, honestly.

Missed blocks. Missed reads. Missed tackles.

But also: flashes.

A perfect drop by George before a pass rusher swallowed him whole — the kind of poised, balanced step-back you couldn't teach, only refine. A textbook seal block by Luis that would've sprung the play if the running back had trusted it. A defensive stand where all eleven players lined up correctly, communicated, and held their ground for four straight snaps. Little moments. Quiet ones. But real.

Cy leaned forward, elbows on his knees, eyes narrowed at the frozen frame on the wall. "There's something here," he said quietly, almost to himself.

Dwyer didn't look away from the screen. He just nodded once. "Yeah. Buried under a whole lot of 'not yet,' but it's there."

They kept going. Rewinding. Pausing. Scribbling notes on a legal pad already scarred with arrows, circles, and question marks. They argued over footwork, over gap assignments, over whether a certain kid was ready for more responsibility or needed to be protected from it. They weren't frustrated — not tonight. They were engaged. Energized. Two men staring at a mess and seeing the outline of something that could become a team.

By the time they shut the projector off, the shed felt smaller, warmer, like the air itself had thickened with possibility. They had another plan — not a miracle cure, not even close, but a new direction. A way to chip at the mountain instead of standing at the bottom of it.

Wednesday's practice was sharper. Louder. The kind of loud that comes from kids who suddenly believe their effort matters. By Friday, the Midgets were hitting sleds with enough force to rattle the bolts, the metal groaning under the strain of boys who'd decided they weren't going to be pushed around anymore.

They weren't fixed. They weren't suddenly contenders.

But they were fighting.

And for a team that had spent too many weeks absorbing punches, that fight — raw, imperfect, stubborn — was the first real sign that something inside them had shifted.

SPIRIT ON THE SIDELINES

Week Four came and went with a familiar sting. Both the Pony Raiders and the Midget Raiders showed real improvement on the road — cleaner blocking, fewer blown assignments, and a level of toughness that hadn't been there in September. But improvement wasn't the same as victory. The East Valley teams they faced were older programs, deeper, and more polished. The Ponies hung close until the fourth quarter before fading. The Midgets battled hard but never quite closed the gap.

Still, Cy saw something different in the boys when they returned to Whitman Field that Monday. They weren't dragging. They weren't defeated. They were learning how to compete.

And that was when an unexpected idea walked right up to him.

Her name was Kelly Donahue, mother of Tyler — a wiry, fast Pony receiver who had quietly become one of Stosh's most reliable kids. Kelly had been a high school cheerleader back in the early '60s, the kind who still remembered every chant, every formation, every Friday night under the lights.

She approached Cy after practice, arms crossed, eyes sharp with purpose.

"Cy, these boys are working their tails off," she said. "They're getting better every week. But they could use something on the sidelines. Something to lift them when things get tough."

Cy raised an eyebrow. "What are you thinking?"

"A cheer squad," she said simply. "For both teams. Something small to start. A dozen girls, maybe. I can run tryouts. I can teach them the basics. And I think the boys would love it."

Cy didn't need long to decide. The league was growing faster than he'd imagined, and the community was leaning in with both shoulders.

"Kelly," he said, "you've got my blessing. Build it."

Her smile told him she'd been waiting for that answer.

Word spread quickly — faster than Cy expected. By Wednesday afternoon, more than thirty girls from town showed up behind the bleachers, some in gym shorts, some in skirts, some in whatever they'd grabbed from their closets. Kelly stood at the front with a whistle, a clipboard, and the unmistakable energy of someone who had just rediscovered a part of herself.

She put them through motions, jumps, claps, and simple chants. Some girls were naturals. Some were enthusiastic. Some were simply thrilled to be part of something.

By the end of the hour, Kelly had her squad: twelve girls, ages twelve to fourteen, eager, loud, and ready to represent the Raiders.

They practiced every evening that week, learning a handful of cheers and a simple halftime routine. Kelly drilled them with the same intensity Stosh used on the Pony offensive line. And the girls responded.

Saturday brought perfect football weather and the biggest crowd Whitman Field had seen all season. Parents filled the bleachers. Younger siblings ran along the fence. The Pee Wee teams played their morning games, a chaotic mix of oversized helmets and tiny legs — the future of the program humming steadily in the background.

But the real show began when the cheer squad took their place near midfield, pom-poms shaking with nervous excitement before the Raiders' games.

"R-A-I-D-E-R-S! Let's go, Raiders!"

The Ponies fed off the energy immediately. Tom caught a swing pass on the second play of the game and turned it into a twenty-yard gain. Marcus punched in a touchdown two drives later. The defense swarmed. The cheer squad kept the crowd loud.

But midway through the third quarter, the game stopped cold.

A visiting running back took a handoff, cut left, and was hit cleanly by two Pony defenders. He went down awkwardly — too awkwardly — and didn't get up.

The field went silent.

Coaches rushed out. Parents leaned forward. Even the cheer squad froze.

Tom jogged over, heart pounding. He'd seen kids get shaken up before, but this felt different. When he reached the cluster of players and coaches, he saw the boy clutching his leg, face pale, eyes wide with pain.

Then Tom saw it — the kneecap, shifted grotesquely to the side.

His stomach flipped.

He stepped back, suddenly aware of how fragile everything was. How one wrong step, one unlucky angle, could change everything. He'd never thought about it before. Football had always been fun, exciting, something he loved without question.

Now, for the first time, he felt the danger.

He forced himself to breathe, to steady his thoughts. The trainers worked quickly, stabilizing the boy and calling for help. When the injured player was finally taken off the field, the crowd applauded softly.

Tom jogged back to the huddle, trying to push the image out of his mind. Trying to be a football player again.

The Ponies regrouped. They drove the field. They scored again. And when the final whistle blew, they had their second win of the season — their first at home.

The Midgets' game followed. From the opening whistle, something felt different. The Midgets flew to the ball, hit clean, wrapped up, and played with a confidence Cy hadn't seen before. Every good play was met with a burst of cheers. Every mistake was drowned out by encouragement.

Late in the fourth quarter, clinging to a six-point lead, the Midgets forced a fumble and recovered it. The sideline erupted — players, parents, cheerleaders, everyone.

When the clock hit zero, the Midgets had their first win of the season.

As the boys celebrated, the cheer squad chanted louder than ever. Parents clapped. Coaches exchanged relieved nods.

And everywhere around Whitman Field, people whispered the same thing:

"Maybe it's the cheerleaders." "Maybe that's what they needed." "Maybe that's the difference."

Some parents swore it was the cheer squad. Others said the boys had simply grown up. Cy knew the truth was somewhere in the middle. Whatever it was, the Raiders were growing — on the field, on the sideline, and in the stands.

The program wasn't just surviving anymore; it was maturing and becoming something real.

Tom, however, didn't sleep well Saturday night.

He kept seeing the boy's leg — the angle, the kneecap shifted to the side, the shock in the kid's eyes. It replayed in flashes, like a film reel he couldn't shut off. He'd always known football was rough. He'd taken his share of hits, gotten the wind knocked out of him, scraped elbows, bruised ribs.

But this was different.

This was real.

By Sunday morning, he tried to push it out of his mind. He tossed a football in the backyard, ran a few routes by himself, tried to feel normal again. But every time he planted his foot, he felt a flicker of doubt.

What if that happened to me?

He hated the thought. Hated that it made him hesitate. Hated that it made him feel small.

But he also knew he couldn't ignore it.

When the Ponies gathered again at Whitman Field, the mood was lighter than usual. Two wins had a way of lifting everything — shoulders, voices, even the way the boys carried their helmets. The cheer squad practiced on the far sideline, working on timing and chants for next week. Parents chatted in small clusters.

But Tom wasn't himself.

Stosh noticed immediately.

"You good?" he asked quietly as Tom stretched.

Tom nodded too quickly. "Yeah. Fine."

Stosh didn't push. He knew when a kid needed space to sort something out. But he also knew when to keep an eye on one.

Across the field, the Midgets were buzzing. Their first win had lit something inside them — not cockiness, but belief. They hit the sleds harder. They ran pursuit drills with sharper angles. They talked more, encouraged more, corrected each other without waiting for a coach.

Cy watched them with quiet satisfaction. Wins didn't fix everything, but they revealed who a team could become.

And this team — this scrappy, undersized, stubborn group — was starting to believe in itself.

Halfway through practice, during a water break, Tom drifted toward Cy. He didn't mean to. His feet just carried him there.

Cy noticed the look — the kind of look he'd seen on dozens of boys since this all began, the look that came after a hard hit or a scary moment.

"You want to talk?" Cy asked.

Tom hesitated. Then he nodded.

"It was bad," Tom said quietly. "His knee. I've never seen anything like that."

Cy didn't sugarcoat it. "It happens. Football's a tough game. Sometimes kids get hurt."

Tom swallowed. "What if it happens to me?"

Cy took a breath. He didn't want to lie. He didn't want to scare him either.

"Tom, every sport has risks. Every kid who steps on a field knows that. But you play the game the right way — with good technique, with your head up, with your body under control — and you lower those risks. You can't play scared. But you can play smart."

Tom nodded slowly. He didn't feel fixed. But he felt steadier.

"Thanks, Dad — I mean, Coach."

"Anytime."

As practice wrapped up, the cheer squad ran through their halftime routine. It wasn't perfect — a few girls were out of sync, one dropped a pom-pom, another forgot a step — but the energy was there. The parents clapped. The boys pretended not to watch but absolutely watched.

Kelly Donahue blew her whistle and reset the formation.

"We'll get it," she said. "We're Raiderettes now. We don't quit."

Cy smiled. The program was becoming bigger than football. Bigger than wins and losses. It was becoming a place where kids — all kids — could belong.

As the sun dipped behind the trees, Tom walked off the field with his helmet under his arm. He still felt the weight of what he'd seen. But he also felt something else — resolve.

He wasn't quitting. He wasn't backing down. He was learning what it meant to be a football player.

And for the Raiders — Ponies, Midgets, and Pee Wees alike — Week Six was coming fast.

THE ROAD THROUGH COALTON HEIGHTS

Two days later was the final practice before the next game, and Cy stood at the edge of the field as the boys trickled in. There was a different energy in the air — not fear, not nerves, but a sharpened awareness. Word had spread about the injury in the Pony game. Kids talked in low voices. Parents lingered a little longer before walking back to their cars.

Football suddenly felt heavier.

Cy watched his son closely. Tom wasn't rattled, not exactly — but something in him had shifted. He moved with more intention. He listened harder. He stretched longer. He wasn't just playing anymore.

He was preparing.

Cy recognized that look. He'd worn it himself once.

Week Six meant facing the Coalton Heights Ironmen, a team known for speed, trick plays, and a coach who loved nothing more than catching opponents asleep. The Ironmen weren't the biggest roster in the league, but they were slippery — the kind of team that turned broken plays into touchdowns.

Cy gathered the coaches near the shed.

"We tighten everything," he said. "Angles, tackling, communication. No freelancing this week."

Dwyer nodded. "Midgets need to clean up their reads. They're still biting on every fake."

Stosh cracked his knuckles. "Ponies'll be ready. Tom's locked in. The whole squad is."

Cy believed him. The Ponies had shown grit in Week Five, and the win at home had lit a spark. People were even whispering that maybe — just maybe — the cheer squad had made the difference. The girls had shown up louder, sharper, more synchronized than in practice. And the boys had fed off it.

Cy didn't know if that was true, but he wasn't about to argue with momentum.

During warmups, Tom ran every drill like it mattered. When a teammate missed an assignment, he didn't snap — he corrected. When someone slacked, he nudged them back into focus. He wasn't trying to be a leader.

He just was.

But every so often, his eyes drifted to the far end of the field — to the spot where the visiting player had gone down the week before. Cy noticed. He walked over, hands in his pockets.

"You good?" he asked.

Tom nodded, but it wasn't convincing.

Cy waited.

Finally, Tom exhaled. "I keep seeing it. His knee. The way he yelled."

Cy didn't sugarcoat it. "It's part of the game. Doesn't happen often, but it can. You learn from it. You respect it. And you keep going."

Tom swallowed. "I'm trying."

"That's all you can do."

But Cy still wondered how this might affect Tom in the next game.

The Raiders caravanned south on Saturday morning, a line of cars winding through the backroads toward Coalton Heights — a town built on steel, grit, and the kind of pride that made youth football feel like a civic duty. Cy drove with his window cracked, letting in the cool air as Tom sat beside him, helmet in his lap, staring out at the passing fields.

He hadn't said much all morning.

The injury from Week Five still lived somewhere behind his eyes.

Ahead of them waited tough opponents. Both Coalton Heights teams were known for being physical, disciplined, and nearly unbeatable on their home field.

It was going to be a long day.

The Coalton Heights field sat in a natural bowl, ringed by tall pines that swallowed sound and sunlight. The Raiders stepped off the bus and felt the weight of the place immediately — quiet, cold, and unfriendly.

Tom jogged through warmups, but his movements were stiff. His eyes kept drifting to the far sideline where Coalton Heights' trainers stretched their players. Every time a knee bent awkwardly or a player stumbled, Tom flinched.

Stosh noticed.

But he didn't say anything yet.

The Ironmen came out firing. Their running back — a stocky kid with tree-trunk legs — barreled through the line again and again. The Ponies tackled high, tackled late, or didn't tackle at all.

Tom was the worst of them.

He hesitated. He reached instead of wrapping. Twice he pulled up entirely, letting someone else make the stop.

By the end of the first quarter, the Ponies trailed 12–0.

Cy paced the sideline, jaw tight. Stosh kept his arms folded, watching Tom more than the scoreboard.

Midway through the second quarter, the Ponies finally forced a fumble. The ball bounced right toward Tom — a gift, a chance to flip momentum.

He froze.

Another Raider dove past him and fell on it, but the moment told Stosh everything he needed to know.

Tom wasn't playing football.

He was playing scared.

The Ponies scraped together a field goal before halftime, but they jogged to the locker room down 12–3, shoulders slumped, confidence leaking away.

The Coalton Heights visitor's locker room was small, wooden, and smelled like old sweat. The boys sat on the benches, helmets at their feet, breathing hard.

Tom sat alone at the end of the row, staring at the floor.

Stosh walked in slowly, not yelling, not pacing. He stood in the center of the room and waited until every eye was on him.

Then he spoke — quietly.

"Football isn't safe," he said. "It never has been. You can get hurt. You can see things you don't want to see. But that's not what defines you."

He looked directly at Tom.

"What defines you is what you do next."

Tom swallowed hard.

Stosh continued. "You think courage means not being scared? Wrong. Courage is being scared and doing your job anyway. You don't run from it. You meet it. You look it in the eye and say, 'Not today.'"

The room was silent.

"You boys earned the right to be here. Now earn the right to finish."

Something inside Tom shifted — not a sudden burst of bravery, but a steadying. A grounding. A decision.

He stood up.

"I'm good," he said.

And this time, he meant it.

From the first snap of the third quarter, Tom was different.

He attacked the line. He wrapped and drove. He shed blocks. He chased down plays from behind. On one crucial third-and-short, he met the Ironmen's big running back head-on, squared up, and dropped him for a loss.

The sideline erupted.

Cy felt his chest loosen for the first time all day.

Down 12–10 with two minutes left, the Ponies started at midfield. Tom made two key blocks on sweeps, then caught a short pass and fought for extra yards, dragging defenders with him.

With twenty seconds left, the Ponies lined up for a short field goal.

The kick sailed just inside the right upright.

13–12.

The Raiders held on defense, and when the final whistle blew, Tom lifted his helmet high, lungs burning, heart pounding — not from fear, but from pride.

He'd faced the thing that haunted him.

And he'd beaten it.

The Ponies had won their second straight game, and another one on the road. Their record was now 3–3

— something to be proud of in their first year in the league.

The Midgets took the field next against the Coalton Heights Ironmen Midgets, a team known for punishing line play and a quarterback who could throw a spiral through a brick wall.

From the start, it was a slugfest.

Dwyer's boys fought hard — harder than they had all season — trading scores, forcing punts, answering every punch with one of their own. But the Ironmen were just a little sharper, a little stronger, a little more seasoned.

Late in the fourth quarter, down 20–14, the Midgets drove to the Ironmen 25-yard line. On fourth and six, their quarterback rolled right, found a receiver open — and the ball slipped through the kid's hands.

Game over.

The Midgets walked off the field exhausted, frustrated, but not defeated. They were close. Closer than expected.

They just couldn't finish it.

As the sun set over Coalton Heights, the Raiders loaded up the bus and accompanying cars for the long ride home. One win. One loss. But something more important than either result lingered in the air.

Growth. Real, undeniable growth.

Tom looked back at the field, jaw set. "I wasn't scared. I just... didn't know it could be like that."

Cy put a hand on his shoulder. "Now you do. And you're still here."

That seemed to settle something inside the boy.

THE ROAD HOME

The inaugural season still had four weeks left, and nobody pretended they'd be easy. But the Raiders — Ponies, Midgets, cheerleaders, coaches, parents — had crossed a line. They weren't guessing anymore. They knew what this league demanded.

And they kept showing up.

For the Ponies' seventh game, Stosh tightened the playbook, simplified the reads, and let the boys play fast. Tom had his best game yet — nothing flashy, just steady, reliable football. A couple of key catches, a downfield block that sprung a long run, and a tackle on special teams that made the sideline erupt.

They won 14–6. Earned every inch.

The Midgets, meanwhile, ran into a buzzsaw — a big, disciplined squad from the west side that punished every mistake. Dwyer kept them fighting, but the game slipped away early and never came back.

Still, something was different. Even in defeat, the boys didn't sag. They kept hitting, kept hustling, kept learning.

Week Eight was all about the Midgets. Dwyer's boys came out sharp — quick passes, misdirection runs, and a defense that swarmed like hornets. They forced turnovers, capitalized on field position, and controlled the clock. It wasn't pretty, but it was tough, smart football.

They won 20–13.

The Ponies, on the other hand, stumbled. A couple of early turnovers put them behind, and they never quite recovered. Tom played well, but the team couldn't find rhythm. Stosh kept them composed, though, and the boys walked off with their heads up.

During Week Nine, both teams hit a wall.

The Ponies lost a heartbreaker — 7–0 in a defensive slugfest where one busted coverage made the difference. Tom took it personally, replaying the missed block in his head long after the whistle. Cy talked him through it, the way only a father could.

The Midgets dropped their game too, undone by penalties and missed assignments. Dwyer didn't yell. He didn't need to. The boys knew.

It was the kind of week that tests a program.

And the Raiders didn't break.

The final week brought crisp air, a big crowd for the last home game, and a sense that everyone — players, coaches, parents — understood what this season had really been about.

The Ponies came out swinging. They played loose, confident, almost joyful. Tom caught a touchdown on a simple out-and-up, his feet dancing just inside the sideline. The defense held strong, and they closed the season with a 21–12 win.

Five wins. Five losses. A .500 season that felt like a mountain climbed.

The Midgets wrapped up their year with a gritty, come-from-behind victory — 13–7. A late interception sealed it, and the sideline exploded. Dwyer didn't smile often, but he did then.

They finished 3–7. Not glamorous. But honest. Hard-earned. Real.

The cheerleader squad grew too — more confident, more synchronized, more proud of their place in the Raiders family. They weren't just decoration; they were part of the heartbeat of every Saturday.

The Pee-Wees, meanwhile, had become a small army. Dozens of little kids in oversized helmets chasing flags, learning stances, dreaming big. Tom watched them sometimes and saw himself from just a year ago.

The pipeline was real now. The future was real.

When the final games ended and the lights clicked off for the last time, Cy stood alone on the field for a moment.

He thought about everything they'd survived:

- The early chaos
- The first bruising losses
- The injuries and scares
- The breakthroughs
- The wins that felt like miracles
- The losses that taught more than the wins ever could
- The boys who grew up right in front of him
- His own son, finding courage he didn't know he had

It hadn't been perfect. It hadn't even been pretty most of the time.

But it had been worth it.

The Raiders had a foothold now. A foundation. A reason to believe.

And Cy knew — deep in his bones — that this was only the beginning.

Although the season ended on a cold Saturday, the warmth around the Raiders program didn't fade. If anything, it grew stronger. On that last day, parents lingered longer than normal. Kids stayed to toss the ball under the lights. Coaches talked about next year with a confidence none of them had dared to show in August.

Eventually everyone dispersed, but something felt incomplete. Most everyone sensed it, but nobody could define it.

Later that week, unable to shake the feeling that the boys — and their families — deserved something more meaningful than a wave and a parting nod, Joanne felt a rush of emotion rise inside her.

Out of that came an idea.

"You need a banquet," she told Cy one night as they cleaned up the kitchen. "Not just for the boys — for everyone. Coaches, cheerleaders, Pee-Wees, families. A real celebration. Something that says this mattered."

Cy looked at her, tired but grateful. "You really think people would come? We should be able to cover it — we've actually got more money left than I expected. The concessions alone brought in a small fortune."

"They'll come," she said. "Trust me."

And they did.

Joanne secured the community center on short notice — a big hall with long tables, a small stage, and enough space for every team in the league. She organized volunteers, coordinated food, arranged decorations in Raiders colors, and even convinced a local bakery to donate a massive sheet cake with the Raiders name piped across the top.

When Cy walked in that evening, he stopped in the doorway.

The place was packed.

Parents chatted like old friends. Some of the Ponies chased each other between tables. Cheerleaders practiced a routine in the corner, giggling and shushing each other. The Pee-Wees tore around the room with the boundless, unstoppable energy only pre-teens can muster.

It felt like a family.

Joanne slipped her arm through his. "Told you."

After dinner, Cy stepped onto the small stage. The room quieted, though it took a few taps on the microphone to settle the Pee-Wees.

He started with the awards.

Nothing flashy — just simple plaques and certificates — but each one meant something:

- **Most Improved**
- **Best Teammate**
- **Iron Pony Award**
- **Midget Leadership Award**
- **Cheer Spirit Award**
- **Pee-Wee Heart Award**

Every time a name was called, the room erupted. Kids beamed. Parents wiped their eyes. Coaches clapped like proud uncles.

Tom received the **Commitment Award**, and when he walked up, Cy felt something tighten in his chest. Not pride exactly — something deeper. Recognition. Understanding. The boy had grown.

And he wasn't the only one.

The friendships between players were unmistakable now. Boys who barely knew each other in August were sitting shoulder to shoulder, trading stories, laughing at inside jokes, nudging each other during speeches. They weren't just teammates anymore.

They were a team.

When the awards were done, Joanne gave Cy a small nod from the back of the room. He took a breath, stepped forward, and let the silence settle.

"I don't know if I can put this season into words," he began. "But I'm going to try."

He looked out at the faces — parents who trusted him, coaches who stood beside him, kids who had given everything they had.

"This league started as an idea. A hope. Maybe even a gamble. We didn't know what we were doing half the time. We made mistakes. We learned on the fly. We took our lumps. But every week, you all showed up. You believed in something that didn't exist yet."

He paused, letting the weight of that truth sink in.

"And look at what we built."

He gestured around the room.

"Two teams that fought every week for this town's name. Cheerleaders who brought energy and pride. Pee-Wees who reminded us why we love this game. Coaches who gave their time and their hearts. Parents who supported us even when things got messy."

His voice thickened.

"And kids… you grew. You grew in ways that don't show up on a scoreboard. You learned courage. You learned teamwork. You learned how to get back up. That's what football is. That's what life is."

He swallowed hard.

"I'm proud of every one of you. And I promise you this — we're just getting started."

The applause rose slowly at first, then built into something powerful. Something earned.

As the night wound down, kids clustered in groups, already talking about next season — plays they wanted to try, positions they hoped to earn, teams they wanted to beat. Coaches exchanged ideas. Parents offered to help with fundraising, equipment, transportation.

The Raiders weren't just a league anymore.

They were a community. No — a family.

Joanne stood beside Cy as the last tables were cleared. "You did good," she said softly.

Cy shook his head. "We did good."

She smiled. "Next year's going to be even bigger."

He believed her.

For the first time since the idea of the league had taken root, Cy felt something settle deep inside him — not relief, not exhaustion.

Contentment.

Winter settled in a slow, steady hush. The fields where the Raiders had run and shouted and collided all fall were empty now, the grass brittle and pale under morning frost. But the quiet didn't mean stillness. If anything, the off-season was louder than the games had ever been.

Cy learned quickly that a league didn't sleep. It just changed shape. Two weeks after the banquet, he sat at his kitchen table with a yellow legal pad and a mug of coffee that had gone cold twice already. Joanne had insisted he take a break — "Just a week, Cy. One week without football" — but his mind refused to cooperate.

He scribbled:

- More practice equipment
- Skills clinics
- Coaching workshops
- Sponsorships?

Every idea felt like a door opening. Every door led to three more.

He wasn't alone, either. Coaches called him at all hours with suggestions. Parents sent letters offering help with fundraising, carpentry, or grant writing. One dad even said he knew a guy who knew a guy who could get them discounted turf paint.

The Raiders weren't just growing. They were evolving.

Even in the cold, kids kept showing up at the field. Not for official practices — those were months away — but to run routes, toss a ball, or just be where the season had happened.

Cy drove by one Saturday morning and saw a cluster of them, bundled in hoodies, breath puffing in the air as they ran makeshift drills. No coaches. No whistles. Just pure, unfiltered love of the game.

He parked and watched from his car for a long moment.

This is why we do it, he thought.

Success brings expectations. Cy felt that truth settle on his shoulders as January rolled in. The Raiders had been a miracle the first year — scrappy, chaotic, stitched together with duct tape and goodwill. But now people expected more.

And Cy wanted to deliver. He wanted the Raiders to be something the kids could count on, something the town could be proud of.

But he also knew that growth meant decisions. Hard ones.

Should they add more Pee-Wee teams? More divisions? Should they cap enrollment? Charge admission at games? Sell programs? Try to build a permanent facility?

Every choice felt like a fork in the road.

One evening, Joanne stopped by with a stack of folders under her arm.

"Budget proposals," she said, dropping them on the table. "And a list of grants we might qualify for. And a draft for a sponsorship letter."

Cy blinked. "When did you do all this?"

"While you were pretending to take a break."

He laughed, but she didn't.

"Cy, listen. Last year was about proving the Raiders could exist. This year is about proving it can last."

He knew she was right.

By February, the town was buzzing again. Kids asked when sign-ups would open. Parents asked about volunteer roles. Coaches asked about clinics. Even the high school coach stopped Cy in the grocery store to say, "You're building something real here."

Cy felt the momentum rising like a tide.

The Raiders weren't just coming back.

They were coming back stronger.

And as he stood on the empty field one cold afternoon, hands shoved in his jacket pockets, he could already picture it — the whistles, the cheers, the thud of cleats on grass, the bright jerseys flashing under the sun.

Season Two wasn't here yet.

But it was coming.

And Cy was ready.

But winter didn't just bring planning. It brought reality.

Cy's alarm still went off at four every morning. Coal didn't deliver itself, and the cold months were the busiest of the year. Folks needed heat, and Cy's truck rumbled across the valley from dawn until late afternoon, leaving trails of black dust and the smell of diesel in its wake.

By the time he got home, his shoulders ached, his hands were raw, and his clothes carried the weight of the day. But the Raiders didn't pause just because he was tired.

Some evenings, Cy would drop his work boots by the door, kiss his son on the head, and sit down at the kitchen table only to find Joanne already waiting with a stack of forms or a list of calls he needed to return.

"Just a few things," she'd say.

It was never just a few.

Registration planning. Equipment orders. Volunteer schedules. Insurance forms. Fundraising proposals. Meetings with town officials. Meetings with parents. Meetings with coaches.

Cy felt like he was living two full lives at once.

One paid the bills.

The other fed his soul.

Tom loved the Raiders — loved that his dad had built something everyone talked about — but he also missed him.

One night, as Cy said goodnight, Tom asked, "Dad, can we spend more quality time together? Outside of football, I mean."

The question hit harder than any tackle Cy had ever taken.

"I'll always be here," he said. "Even when I'm busy."

But he wondered if that was true. The league was growing faster than he'd expected. Faster than he'd planned for. And every new idea came with a new responsibility.

Joanne tried to reassure him.

"You're doing something good," she said. "Something that matters."

"I know," Cy replied. "I just don't want to lose us — or Tom — in the process."

The challenges kept stacking.

A neighboring town wanted to join the league, which sounded great until Cy realized it meant more fields, more refs, more scheduling headaches.

A local business offered sponsorship — but only if the Raiders agreed to branding changes Cy wasn't sure he liked.

One coach wanted to run a spring training camp. Another wanted to add a second travel team. A group of parents suggested a flag football division.

Every idea had merit. Every idea required time.

And Cy had only so much of that to give.

One icy morning, after hauling a full load of coal up a steep mountain road, Cy sat in the cab of his truck and stared at the valley below. The sun was rising, turning the frost on the fields into a glittering sheet of silver.

He should've felt proud.

Instead, he felt overwhelmed.

"What if I can't keep up?" he muttered. "What if last year was a fluke?"

The fear surprised him. He hadn't felt it during the season — not once. But now, with the quiet pressing in, the doubts had room to breathe.

That afternoon, as he drove past the Raiders' field, he saw something that eased the knot in his chest.

A group of kids — maybe a dozen — were out there again, bundled in mismatched jackets and gloves, running plays in the cold. No adults. No structure. Just joy.

One kid threw a pass that wobbled through the air. Another dove for it, landing hard on the frozen ground. They all laughed.

Cy pulled over again and watched.

This — this was the heart of it. Not the paperwork. Not the meetings. Not the stress.

The kids.

The community.

The belief that something small could grow into something lasting.

He took a deep breath, letting the cold air clear his head.

Season Two was going to be bigger. Harder. Busier.

But it was also going to be worth it.

Cy put the truck back in gear and drove on, feeling the weight on his shoulders shift — not gone, but steadier.

He wasn't doing this alone.

And he wasn't done yet.

February brought more than cold winds.

It brought a blow Cy didn't see coming.

It started with a cough — deep, rattling, the kind that shook his ribs. He ignored it at first. Coal dust had been part of his life since he was sixteen. A cough was just a cough.

But then came the shortness of breath. The tightness in his chest after climbing into the truck. The way he had to pause halfway up the porch steps, pretending he'd forgotten something so his family wouldn't see him catching his breath.

Joanne noticed.

"You're wheezing," she said one night as he unlaced his boots.

"It's nothing."

"It's not nothing."

She made him promise to see a doctor. He didn't want to — time off meant deliveries piling up, customers calling, bills waiting — but the next morning, halfway through unloading a half-ton of coal, he felt a sharp, burning pain under his ribs that forced him to his knees.

He sat there in the cold, breath fogging in front of him, heart pounding too fast.

That's when he knew he couldn't ignore it anymore.

The clinic smelled like antiseptic and old magazines. Cy sat on the exam table, hands clasped, feeling like a kid waiting to be scolded.

The doctor listened to his lungs, frowned, listened again.

"You've got inflammation from long-term dust exposure," he said. "Your lungs are irritated. You need rest. Real rest. No exceptions."

Cy nodded, but his stomach twisted.

Rest wasn't an option. Not in winter. Not with the Raiders growing. Not with a family depending on his coal deliveries.

The doctor must've seen the conflict on his face.

"You keep pushing like this," he said gently, "and you won't make it to next season."

The words hit harder than the pain had.

That night, Cy sat at the kitchen table long after everyone else had gone to bed. The house was quiet except for the hum of the refrigerator and the occasional creak of settling wood.

He stared at the inhaler the doctor had given him.

He thought about the coal truck. The Raiders. His family. The future he was trying to build.

He felt pulled in every direction, stretched thin enough to tear.

For the first time in a long time, he wondered if he was in over his head.

The next day, Joanne stopped by with more paperwork — but she took one look at him and set the stack aside.

"You look awful," she said bluntly.

"Thanks."

"What's going on?"

Cy hesitated. He didn't like talking about himself. Didn't like admitting weakness. But Joanne wasn't just a volunteer anymore. She was part of the backbone of the Raiders.

So he told her.

When he finished, she didn't say anything for a long moment.

Then: "Cy… you can't run this league alone."

"I'm not alone."

"You're acting like you are."

He opened his mouth to argue, but she held up a hand.

"Let us help. Let me help. Delegate. Trust people. If you burn out, the whole thing collapses."

He hated how right she was.

Over the next week, Cy forced himself to slow down. He let the other drivers take more of the heavy routes. He let Joanne handle the sponsorship calls. He let Coach Johnson organize the spring clinic. He let a player's mom take over the fundraising committee.

It wasn't easy. Every instinct told him to do more, push harder, carry the weight himself.

But little by little, the load lightened.

And something unexpected happened.

The league didn't fall apart.

It grew stronger.

One evening, as Cy stood on the porch watching the sun dip behind the hills, Joanne slipped her arm around his waist.

"You don't have to be everything," she said softly.

"I know."

"You just have to be here."

He nodded, breathing in the cool air — slowly, carefully, but without pain.

The setback had scared him. It had humbled him. But it had also forced him to see the truth:

The Raiders weren't his burden to carry.

They were a community to build.

And he wasn't building it alone.

THE SEASON OF LEANING ON OTHERS

C y woke earlier than usual the next morning, not because of an alarm, but because his body had decided it was done sleeping. He sat on the edge of the bed for a moment, letting the quiet settle around him. The scare had shaken him more deeply than he wanted to admit. Joanne had seen it. Tom had sensed it. And Cy... well, he was still sorting through what it meant.

He padded downstairs, careful not to wake anyone, and poured himself a glass of water. No coffee today. Joanne's orders. Doctor's orders. His own common sense, if he was being honest.

The house felt different in the early light — still, grounded, almost expectant. As if it knew he was at a crossroads.

He leaned against the counter and let the truth settle in again.

He didn't have to carry everything. He didn't have to fix everything. He didn't have to be everything.

The league didn't need a savior. It needed a leader who knew when to ask for help.

And Cy was ready to continue doing that.

He grabbed the notebook he'd been scribbling in for months — practice plans, equipment lists, budgets, dreams — and flipped to a clean page. At the top, he wrote one word:

Delegation.

It looked strange in his handwriting, like it belonged to someone more organized, more patient, more reasonable. But he kept writing:

- Stosh: defensive drills, conditioning
- Dwyer: equipment inventory, ordering
- Joe: sponsorships, fundraising
- Joanne: scheduling, communication
- Parents: field setup, cleanup, concessions

He stared at the list. It wasn't complicated. It wasn't revolutionary. It was just… shared.

And it felt right.

A soft creak came from the stairs. Joanne appeared, tying her robe, eyes still heavy with sleep but sharp enough to read him instantly.

"You're up early," she said.

"Couldn't sleep."

She stepped closer, studying him. "How do you feel?"

"Better," he said. And he meant it. "Clearer."

She nodded slowly. "Good. Because you scared us."

"I scared myself," he admitted.

Joanne reached out and touched his arm. "Then let's not do that again."

He smiled. "Deal."

She glanced at the notebook. "What's that?"

"A new plan," he said. "A smarter one."

She raised an eyebrow. "Smarter how?"

"I'm not doing this alone anymore."

Her expression softened into something warm and relieved. "About time."

Cy closed the notebook. "I'm going to call Stosh today. And Dwyer. And maybe Joe. I want to get ahead of things before the summer hits."

"Good," she said. "But pace yourself."

"I will."

She gave him a look that said she'd hold him to it.

Cy walked to the window and looked out at the quiet street. Kids would be riding their bikes there soon. Parents would be talking about sign-ups. The town would start buzzing again. And when it did, he wanted to be ready.

The scare was still fresh in his mind, but he was easing into his new approach — slower mornings, shared responsibilities, and a league that didn't rest entirely on his shoulders.

Then, in early March, the challenge arrived.

Not with a phone call. Not with a letter. But with a knock. A hard, urgent knock on the front door just after breakfast.

Cy opened it to find Paul Dwyer, hat in hand, breathing like he'd jogged the whole way.

"Cy," he said, "you better come down to Whitman Field."

Cy's stomach tightened. "What happened?"

Paul shook his head. "Just… come."

Cy grabbed his coat, told Joanne he'd be back, and followed Paul down the street. They didn't talk. Paul's silence said enough.

When they reached the field, Cy saw the problem immediately. The irrigation ditch behind the far end zone had collapsed.

A winter thaw followed by heavy rain had washed out a ten-foot section of the bank. The ground had slumped inward, leaving a jagged, muddy crater that chewed halfway into the back corner of the field.

Stosh was already there, boots sunk in the muck, hands on his hips.

"Damn thing gave way sometime last night," he said. "I came by to check the shed and found this."

Cy stepped closer, careful not to slide. The damage was worse up close. The ditch had been old to begin with — hand-dug decades earlier when Earl Whitman still farmed the land. Years of runoff had eaten at it, and now it had finally given out.

"How bad?" Cy asked.

Stosh shrugged. "Bad enough. We can't run practices like this. Kids'll break their necks."

Paul added, "And Earl's not gonna be thrilled. This is his land. He's always been nervous about us being here."

That hit Cy harder than the washout itself. Earl Whitman had given them the field on trust — cautious, conditional trust. If he saw the damage and decided the league was more trouble than it was worth…

Cy exhaled slowly. Old Cy would've jumped straight into the hole with a shovel. Old Cy would've tried to fix it himself, sunup to sundown, until his back gave out.

But that Cy had nearly put himself in the ground.

He looked at Stosh and Paul. "Alright. Let's think."

Stosh blinked. "You're… thinking?"

"Trying something new," Cy said.

Paul smirked. "About time."

Cy crouched near the edge of the washout. "We need the ditch rebuilt. Reinforced. Proper drainage. This isn't a rake-and-shovel job."

Stosh nodded. "We'll need equipment."

"And people," Paul added. "A lot of them."

Cy stood. "Then we get them."

By noon, Cy had walked the entire neighborhood, knocking on familiar doors, talking to parents, shop owners — anyone with tools, machinery, or know-how.

Some offered shovels. Some offered time. One offered a backhoe — if they could get it running.

But the biggest surprise came from Earl Whitman himself. He showed up at the field late in the afternoon, hands in his coat pockets, eyes narrowed at the damage.

Cy braced for the worst.

Earl grunted. "Damn ditch has been a problem since '62."

Cy blinked. "You're… not upset?"

"Oh, I'm upset," Earl said. "But not at you. Land shifts. Water wins. Always has."

He kicked a clod of mud. "You boys fix it right, and I'll see about getting you some gravel from the quarry. Might as well do it proper."

Cy felt something loosen in his chest. "We'll fix it."

Earl nodded once. "I know."

Over the next week, Whitman Field became a worksite.

Farmers brought tractors.

A retired mason showed up with forms and rebar.

Kids hauled buckets of gravel.

Moms brought sandwiches and thermoses of coffee.

Earl supervised like a foreman who'd been waiting twenty years for someone to care about this land again.

And Cy? He worked — but not like before.

He didn't lead every task. He didn't micromanage. He didn't push himself past the edge.

He delegated. He trusted. He paced.

And the ditch got rebuilt — stronger, straighter, safer than it had ever been.

On the final day, as they packed up tools, Earl walked over to Cy.

"You handled this well," Earl said.

Cy shrugged. "Didn't do it alone."

"That's the point," Earl replied. "A man who tries to fix everything himself usually ends up breaking something else."

Cy knew exactly what he meant.

Earl stuck out his hand. "You boys can stay on this land as long as you want. I've been watching. You've earned it."

Cy shook his hand, feeling the weight of the moment. The first big test of the off-season hadn't been the ditch. It had been whether Cy could let others carry the load.

For a few weeks, things felt steady.

Then came the envelope.

A plain, cream-colored envelope slid through the mail slot one Thursday afternoon in late March. No return address. Just his name written in a tight, careful hand.

Cy didn't think much of it at first. Bills, notices, church flyers — half the mail looked like this. But when he opened it, a folded letter fell out along with a single sheet of carbon-copy paper.

He unfolded the letter.

It was from **the East Valley Inter-City League Board.**

And it wasn't good.

The board was "reviewing divisional alignments for the upcoming season." They were "concerned about competitive balance." They were "evaluating whether the Raiders program was properly placed."

Cy read the lines twice, then a third time.

They were considering **dropping the Raiders from the league.**

Not because of behavior. Not because of safety. But because they didn't think the Raiders could compete.

It wasn't an insult.

It was worse.

It was pity.

He felt heat rise in his chest. Not anger — something deeper. Something that touched every hour he'd spent building this thing from nothing.

He read the final paragraph: *"We invite you to attend the April board meeting to discuss the matter."*

Cy set the letter down and stared at it.

This was now the real test of his new resolve. Not a ditch or a broken piece of land. This was the league questioning whether the Raiders belonged.

And the old Cy — the one who tried to shoulder everything — would've marched into that meeting ready to fight every board member in the room.

But that Cy was gone.

Or at least, he was supposed to be.

That evening, Cy gathered Stosh, Dwyer, and Joe in his living room. Joanne sat in, too — she always did when something mattered.

Cy handed them the letter.

Stosh read it and muttered, "They think we're weak."

Dwyer shook his head. "They think we're new."

Joe added, "They're protecting their own. They don't want the established teams getting embarrassed if we get good."

Joanne looked at Cy. "What do you want to do?"

He didn't answer right away.

Because the truth was, he didn't know.

He wanted to fight. He wanted to defend the kids. He wanted to prove the board wrong. But he also knew that walking in hot-headed would only confirm their fears.

Finally, he said, "We go to the meeting. All of us."

Stosh raised an eyebrow. "All of us?"

"Yes," Cy said. "If they're evaluating the program, they need to see the program. Not just me."

Dwyer nodded slowly. "Strength in numbers."

Joe added, "And we bring the facts. Participation numbers. Equipment upgrades. Field improvements. Everything."

Joanne smiled. "That's the Cy I like."

Cy exhaled. "I'm not fighting them. I'm showing them who we are."

As the meeting approached, word spread — quietly, but steadily — through town. Parents asked questions. Kids overheard whispers. Earl Whitman stopped by the field one afternoon and said, "You tell that board this land isn't going anywhere."

The community wasn't just behind the Raiders.

They were invested.

And that changed everything.

Cy realized something important: This wasn't about divisions. This wasn't about standings. This wasn't even about football.

This was about legitimacy.

About whether the Raiders were seen as a real program, not a charity case or a novelty.

And the board meeting would decide that.

The night before the board meeting, Cy found Tom in the backyard, tossing a football straight up into the air and catching it against his chest. Over and over. The kind of mindless repetition kids fall into when something's weighing on them.

Cy stepped outside, the screen door creaking behind him. "You'll wear the laces off doing that."

Tom caught the ball and shrugged. "Just practicing."

Cy sat on the back step. "You're thinking about the meeting."

Tom hesitated, then nodded. "The guys at school said the league might drop us. They said it means we're not good enough."

Cy felt that one. Kids always heard things before adults wanted them to.

He patted the step beside him. Tom sat.

"Listen," Cy said, "what league you play in doesn't make a team good or bad. Work does. Heart does. Showing up does."

Tom looked down at the ball in his hands. "But it feels like they don't believe in us."

Cy took a breath. "Then we show them why they should."

Tom glanced up. "You're not mad?"

"I was," Cy admitted. "But being mad doesn't help the boys. Or the program. Or me."

Tom studied him for a long moment. "You're different lately."

Cy smiled. "Trying to be."

Tom nodded slowly, as if deciding something. "If they drop us… I'll still play. We'll find another league or make our own."

That hit Cy harder than he expected. "That's heart… so proud of you."

Tom tossed the ball lightly, catching it with a soft thump. "You're gonna do good tomorrow."

Cy put a hand on his shoulder. "We're gonna do good. All of us."

For the first time all week, Tom smiled.

The League held its monthly meetings in the basement of the old municipal building — fluorescent lights, metal folding chairs, a chalkboard with half-erased notes from some long-forgotten committee.

Cy arrived with Stosh, Dwyer, Joe, and Joanne. They didn't walk in like a delegation.

They walked in like a team.

The board members were already seated behind a long table. Clipboards. Stacks of papers. Coffee in Styrofoam cups. The usual.

Chairman Frank Leland cleared his throat. "Mr. Mozatta, thank you for coming."

Cy nodded. "Thank you for having us."

Frank glanced at the others. "I see you brought your staff."

"My partners," Cy corrected gently.

A few board members exchanged looks.

Frank folded his hands. "As you know, we're reviewing placements for the upcoming season. The Raiders struggled last year. We're concerned about competitive balance."

Cy didn't flinch. "We struggled because we were new. Not because we were incapable."

Another board member, Mrs. Hanley, adjusted her glasses. "We're not questioning your effort. But the scores were… lopsided."

Stosh leaned forward. "Scores don't tell the whole story."

Frank raised a hand. "Let's keep this orderly."

Cy stepped in before Stosh could say more. "We're not here to argue. We're here to show you what we've built since last season."

He opened the folder Joanne had prepared.

Participation numbers. Equipment upgrades. Conditioning plans. Field improvements — complete with photos of a rebuilt ditch and the community turnout. He laid each sheet on the table, one by one.

"We're not the same program you saw last fall," Cy said. "We've grown. The kids have grown. The town has grown around us."

Mrs. Hanley studied the photos. "This is… impressive."

Joe added, "We had thirty-two volunteers out there. On a Saturday. No one asked them. They just came."

Dwyer said, "And we've got commitments from three new sponsors."

Frank tapped the papers. "This is all good. But the question remains — can your boys compete at the current level?"

Cy didn't answer immediately. He let the silence settle. Then he said, "They deserve the chance to prove it."

The room went still. Not defiant. Not confrontational. Just true.

Frank leaned back, exhaling through his nose. "We'll take this under advisement."

Mrs. Hanley added, "We'll notify you by mail within two weeks."

Cy nodded. "Thank you."

As they stood to leave, Frank said, "Mr. Mozatta… it's clear your program has heart."

Cy met his eyes. "It has more than that. It has people."

Frank didn't argue.

The board's decision would arrive soon — another envelope, another turning point. But the real story was that Cy didn't fight alone, didn't lose his temper, didn't try to carry the whole program on his back.

He led.

And the board saw it.

The letter arrived in early May. Same cream-colored envelope. Same tight handwriting. Same quiet weight.

Cy opened it at the kitchen table while Joanne folded laundry nearby. He didn't say anything at first — just read, then read again.

Joanne looked up. "Well?"

He handed it to her.

She scanned the page, then smiled. "They kept us in."

Cy nodded. "No drop."

The news spread fast — through bikes, porches, and word of mouth.

Tom heard it from a friend at school. By the time Cy arrived home later that afternoon, half a dozen boys were already there, tossing a ball around, buzzing with energy.

"Coach!" one of them shouted. "We're staying in the league, right?"

Cy smiled. "That's what the letter says."

The boys erupted — not wild celebration, but something deeper. Pride. Belonging. A sense that they weren't just playing football — they were part of something real.

Tom jogged over. "So we're not just a starter team anymore?"

Cy shook his head. "We never were."

By mid-June, Joanne had the signup table set up inside the Community Center — folding chairs, clipboards, a cardboard box of forms, and a hand-painted sign that read:

RAIDERS FOOTBALL — SEASON TWO

The first hour brought a trickle. The second, a stream. By the end of the morning, they had more kids than they'd ever expected.

Some were returning. Some were new. Some had watched from the sidelines last year and finally decided to jump in.

Parents lingered longer this time. Asked more questions. Offered help.

One dad said, "I've got a pickup and a trailer. You need anything hauled, I'm your guy."

Another mom said, "I can run concessions. I used to do it for Little League."

Cy stood nearby, watching it all unfold — not as a foreman, but as a witness.

Before long, the first Raiders full-team conditioning and tryout session of Season Two arrived. It was a mid-July Saturday, and the sun was already high by 9 a.m., baking the edges of Whitman Field in a haze of gold and dust. The grass was patchy, the dirt dry, and the air thick with humidity.

But the field was alive.

Forty-two kids. Two teams. One program.

Cy stood at the edge of the field with Stosh and Dwyer, clipboard in hand, stopwatch hanging from his neck. He wasn't barking orders. He wasn't pacing like a drill sergeant. He was watching — really watching.

The boys lined up in rows, Pony squad on one side, Midgets on the other. Some had grown. Some hadn't. Some looked ready. Some looked like they'd spent the summer eating popsicles and dodging pushups.

But they were here. And that mattered.

Stosh blew the whistle. "Ten-yard sprints. On my mark."

The boys took off — some fast, some flailing, some gasping by the third rep.

Dwyer called out, "Water break after five. Don't be heroes."

Cy moved between groups, offering quiet corrections, nods of encouragement, the occasional shoulder tap.

He didn't yell. He didn't lecture. He let the work speak.

Tom was in the middle of the Midget pack, pushing hard, sweat soaking through his shirt. He wasn't the fastest. But he was steady.

Cy watched him for a moment, then turned to the Pony squad. One of the new kids — small, wiry, nervous — was lagging behind. Cy crouched beside him.

"You're not here to win today," he said. "You're here to finish."

The boy nodded, breathing hard. "Okay, Coach."

Cy smiled. "Then let's finish."

After an hour, the boys were spent. Shirts clung to backs. Knees were dusty. The field smelled like effort.

Cy gathered them at midfield.

"You showed up," he said. "That's the first win."

He looked around. "This season won't be easy. You'll get hit. You'll get tired. You'll want to quit."

He paused. "But you won't. Because you're Raiders. And Raiders finish."

The boys didn't cheer. They didn't chant. But they stood taller. And that was enough.

Later that night, the shed at Whitman Field was hot, cramped, and smelled like old chalk and motor oil. Cy, Stosh, and Dwyer sat elbow-to-elbow at the workbench, roster sheets spread out between them, a fan rattling in the corner.

Cy tapped his pencil against the clipboard. "Let's start with the Midget squad."

Stosh nodded. "We've got twelve moving up from last year's Ponies."

Dwyer added, "Eight are solid. Four need a look."

Cy scanned the names:

- **Tom Mozatta**: steady, smart, not flashy but reliable
- **Ricky Bell**: fast, undersized, fearless
- **Jamal Carter**: big frame, raw technique
- **Danny Rizzo**: quiet, consistent, coachable
- **Eddie Fisher**: good hands, needs confidence
- **Leo Wagner**: scrappy, emotional, sometimes too emotional
- **Marcus Flynn**: strong legs, weak lungs
- **Calvin "Beans" McGraw**: utility kid, plays anywhere, never complains

The other four — still growing, still figuring it out. Cy circled them for later discussion.

Then Dwyer slid a separate sheet across the table. "Walk-ons."

Cy read the name at the top.

Tony Matz.

Stosh raised an eyebrow. "That the skinny kid?"

"Showed up with no parents," Dwyer said. "Ran every drill. Didn't say much."

Cy nodded. "I watched him. He's not fast. Not strong. But he doesn't quit."

Stosh leaned back. "He's gonna get flattened."

Cy looked at him. "Then we teach him how to get back up."

Dwyer added, "He's got heart. You can see it."

Cy circled Tony's name. "We've got room. He's in."

The next evening, the boys ran a short scrimmage — half-speed, no pads, just movement and positioning.

Tony lined up at cornerback, knees bent, eyes wide. The receiver across from him was bigger, faster, more confident.

The ball snapped. Tony got beat. Twice. Then again.

But he kept lining up. Kept chasing. Kept trying.

Cy watched from the sideline, arms crossed. He didn't say a word.

After the final rep, Tony jogged off, breathing hard, shirt soaked through.

Cy met him halfway. "You're on the team."

Tony blinked. "Really?"

"You earned it," Cy said. "Not with speed. Not with size. With effort."

Tony nodded, a grin breaking through. "I'll work hard."

"I know you will," Cy said. "That's why you're here."

Later that week, the July heat hadn't let up. By early evening, Whitman Field shimmered like a griddle, and the boys clattered across it in full pads for the first time that summer. Helmets knocked together, chinstraps snapped, and the sound of cleats on dry grass filled the air.

Cy stood with Stosh and Dwyer near the 40-yard line, arms folded, watching the Midget squad jog out. This was the day that separated the kids who liked football from the kids who loved it.

And Tony Matz looked like he was trying to decide which one he was.

His helmet sat a little crooked. His shoulder pads were a set that didn't quite fit. His legs were thin, his stance awkward, and he kept adjusting his chinstrap like it was choking him.

But he was there. And he wasn't hiding.

"Form tackling!" Dwyer barked. "One on one. No heroes."

The boys lined up. Tony ended up across from Jamal Carter — big, raw, and eager to hit something.

Cy winced. "That's a mismatch."

Dwyer shrugged. "Only one way to learn."

The whistle blew.

Jamal came in low and fast. Tony braced, but it was like watching a mailbox try to stop a truck. Jamal wrapped him up clean and drove him backward into the grass.

Tony hit the ground hard — the kind of hit that makes a kid rethink his hobbies.

Cy took a step forward, ready to intervene — but stopped.

Tony rolled over, pushed himself up, and got back in line.

No complaining. No theatrics. Just grit.

Dwyer muttered, "Kid's tougher than he looks."

During water break, Tony sat alone on the sideline, helmet off, hair plastered to his forehead. He looked like he was trying to catch his breath and his courage at the same time.

Tom walked over, carrying two cups of water.

He handed one to Tony. "You okay?"

Tony nodded, though he clearly wasn't.

Tom sat beside him. "Jamal hits everyone like that. Even me."

Tony looked up. "Does it get easier?"

Tom thought about it. "You get better. And then it feels easier."

Tony cracked a small smile. "You're Cy's kid, right?"

"Yeah."

"So you kinda have to be good."

Tom shrugged. "Not really. I just try hard."

Tony looked at him, surprised. "That's what Coach said about me."

Tom nudged him with his shoulder. "Then you're already on the right track."

It wasn't a speech. It wasn't a pep talk. It was just one kid helping another find his footing.

Cy watched from a distance, then shouted, "Bull in the ring!"

The one drill every kid dreaded.

The team formed a tight circle — shoulder pads brushing, cleats digging into the dirt. Dust hung in the air like smoke.

Tony Matz was picked for the middle. Running in place. Knees high. Eyes darting. Breathing fast.

His helmet still sat a little crooked, and his pads looked like they belonged to someone bigger, but he didn't complain. He just kept his feet moving.

Cy walked the outside of the circle, slow and deliberate, tapping each boy's helmet as he passed — not signaling yet, just building the tension.

"Keep those feet hot, Tony," Cy said. "Don't you stop."

Tony nodded, legs pumping.

Cy stopped behind Ricky Bell and tapped his shoulder.

Ricky snapped upright. "HERE!"

Tony spun toward the voice just in time to brace as Ricky burst out of the circle and delivered a clean, hard hit. Tony absorbed it, wrapped up instinctively, and the two of them tumbled into the dirt.

The circle roared.

Tony scrambled up, shaking his head, and went right back to running in place.

Cy didn't give him time to settle.

Another tap.

"HERE!"

Jamal this time — bigger, heavier, faster. Tony squared up, but Jamal's hit drove him back two full steps before he managed to stay on his feet.

The boys howled. Even Dwyer cracked a grin.

Tony staggered, caught himself, and kept running.

Cy circled again, tapping shoulders one by one, each time choosing a different boy — quick ones, strong ones, awkward ones, kids Tony had no business standing up to.

But he did.

Every time.

He got knocked down. He got spun around. He got buried once so deep in the dust that Cy started to step in —

— but Tony popped back up, legs churning, eyes wild and determined.

Cy felt something twist in his chest.

The kid wasn't athletic. He wasn't polished. But he had something you couldn't teach.

Heart. Stubborn, stupid, beautiful heart.

Finally, after what felt like ten straight hits, Cy raised his hand.

"That's enough!"

Tony slowed, wobbling, hands on his knees, gasping for air. His jersey was streaked with dirt. His legs shook. His eyes were watery. Sweat dripped off his chin.

Raider sweat.

But he was smiling.

The circle broke, boys clapping him on the helmet, slapping his back, shouting his name.

"Matz!" "Nice job, man!" "You survived!"

Tony looked like he couldn't believe it.

Cy stepped forward, put a hand on his shoulder pad, and gave it a firm squeeze.

"You earned your place today," he said quietly.

Tony nodded, still catching his breath. "Thank you, Coach."

Cy shook his head. "Don't thank me. You did the work."

After dinner, Cy sat on the back steps with Joanne, the cicadas humming in the trees. He told her about the practice, about Tony, about the hits he took and the way he kept getting up.

Joanne listened, legs tucked under her, eyes soft.

"He reminds me of someone," Cy said.

"Who?" she asked.

"Me," Cy admitted. "When I was his age. Skinny. Scared. Trying to prove I wasn't a mistake on the roster."

Joanne smiled. "You turned out alright."

Cy chuckled. "Still working on it."

She leaned her head on his shoulder. "That's why you're good for these boys. You see the ones who need someone to believe in them."

Cy looked out at the quiet street, thinking of Tony's crooked helmet and stubborn determination.

"He's got something," Cy said. "Not talent. Not yet. But something."

"Heart?" Joanne asked.

"Yeah," Cy said. "And that's the part you can't coach."

A TEST WORTH TAKING

The next few weeks unfolded with a steady, almost methodical rhythm. Nothing rushed. Nothing forced. Just the slow, deliberate shaping of something that felt bigger than football.

Every afternoon, as the late-summer heat settled over the field, the league came alive in layers. Parents parked along the fence line. Younger siblings chased each other in the grass. Coaches barked instructions. Whistles cut through the air. It was messy, noisy, hopeful — the kind of scene Cy had always imagined but never quite believed he'd see.

The Midgets were the first to show real signs of transformation.

Last year's 5–5 record as Ponies had been a lesson in frustration — a team that could look sharp one quarter and lost the next. But now, something was different. Not dramatic. Not overnight. More like a slow tightening of bolts, a gradual sharpening of edges.

Cy noticed it during warmups. Their lines were straighter. Their chatter more focused. They moved with a quiet confidence that hadn't been there before.

During drills, Coach Dwyer pushed them hard — footwork, pursuit angles, timing routes, tackling form. And instead of dragging themselves through it, the boys leaned in. They corrected each other. They asked questions. They stayed after practice to run one more rep.

Tom, quiet as ever, had become the boy everyone watched — not because he talked, but because he never quit. First in line. Last to leave. A steady presence the others naturally followed.

One afternoon, Cy watched them run a full-team pursuit drill. Eleven boys flowed across the field in near-perfect sync, closing on the ball carrier with discipline instead of chaos. It wasn't flashy, but it was real football.

He felt something settle in his chest.

"They're starting to get it," he murmured.

Not just the plays. The idea of being a team.

Down the field, the Pony squad worked through their own growing pains. They were younger, still figuring out how to move as a unit, but Stosh had them improving in small, steady steps.

Behind them, the Pee Wees were a world unto themselves — a tangle of oversized helmets, crooked pads, and boundless energy. Half the time they ran the wrong direction, but every now and then, one of them would execute a perfect handoff or make a clean tackle, and Cy would feel the future of the league flicker to life.

It was all connected — the Midgets sharpening, the Ponies learning, the Pee Wees discovering the game for the first time. A pipeline forming right in front of him.

And then there were the cheerleaders.

What started as a casual suggestion had turned into a full-fledged squad. Twelve girls practicing chants and simple routines near the far end zone. Their voices drifted across the field during drills, adding a new rhythm to the late afternoons. It wasn't polished yet. But it was earnest. And it made the whole operation feel more complete.

Cy would catch glimpses of them between plays — ponytails bouncing, sneakers scuffing the grass, laughter carrying on the breeze — and he'd think, *This is what a league looks like.*

Still, Cy knew practice only told part of the story. Improvement was one thing. Competing was another.

He wanted a real test — something that would show him whether the Midgets' progress was genuine or just the illusion of familiarity.

So he made a call to a coach he knew in Piscataway, New Jersey — a program from a tough neighborhood, known for speed, discipline, and a brand of football that didn't back down. Mostly African American boys, coached hard and proud.

When Cy told Dwyer who he'd scheduled for the first scrimmage, the coach raised an eyebrow.

"That's a big step," Dwyer said.

"That's the point," Cy replied. "If we're going to compete in our own league, I need to know what we really have."

The morning of the scrimmage arrived warm and humid, the kind of day where the air felt thick enough to hold sound in place. The Raiders were already stretching when the Piscataway bus pulled into the lot.

The doors opened, and the visiting team stepped out — tall boys, fast boys, confident boys. Their uniforms were worn but sharp. Their movements had a rhythm the Raiders weren't used to seeing.

The Galesburg kids stared.

Not out of disrespect.

Out of unfamiliarity.

There weren't many African American families in town. Seeing an entire team — strong, loud, laughing, focused — was new. And for a moment, the Raiders froze, unsure how to react.

Cy stepped forward, voice steady.

"Eyes on your work," he said. "They're just boys like you. They sweat the same. They want to win the same. Now show me you belong on the same field."

The Raiders nodded, helmets snapping on with a little more purpose.

The first whistle blew, and Piscataway came out fast. Their running back hit the hole like he'd been launched. Their quarterback threw tight spirals that cut through the air. Their defense swarmed with a kind of practiced aggression the Raiders hadn't faced before.

But the Raiders didn't fold.

They adjusted. Slowly at first, then with growing confidence.

They matched speed with discipline. Matched swagger with grit. Matched big plays with bigger heart.

A long, grinding drive in the second quarter showed what they'd become — twelve plays, mixing power runs with short passes, capped by a perfectly timed counter that sprung their tailback for twenty yards. The sideline erupted. The cheer squad found its voice. The Midgets believed.

Late in the fourth, tied 14–14, Piscataway tried to break the game open with a deep post. But the Raiders' safety — a boy who'd been timid last season — read it clean, broke on the ball, and knocked it away with a fearless hit that sent the sideline roaring.

Two plays later, the Raiders punched in the winning score.

Final: **Raiders 20, Piscataway 14.**

As the boys shook hands at midfield, Cy stood with his arms crossed, watching the exchange. No gloating. No fear. Just mutual respect.

Dwyer stepped beside him. "They surprised me today."

Cy nodded slowly. "They surprised themselves."

He looked out at the boys — sweaty, tired, proud — and felt something shift inside him. Not a prediction. Not a promise.

A possibility.

For the first time all year, he let himself imagine what this season might become.

Although the scrimmage drew a solid crowd, plenty of folks stayed home simply because it was a scrimmage. Maybe they didn't want to get their hopes up — or brace for disappointment — before the season even started. But word of the game spread through Galesburg faster than Cy expected.

By Monday morning, people who had never been to the field were stopping him at the hardware store, the diner, even at the gas pump.

He heard things like:

"Cy, I heard those boys from Jersey were the real deal." "Twenty to fourteen? Our boys did that?" "Maybe this team's gonna be something after all."

It wasn't bragging. It wasn't hype. It was curiosity turning into pride — the kind that had been missing from the town for a long time. Folks were hungry for something to rally around, and the Raiders had given them a spark.

At the Alter Street Café, two older men who'd coached Little League decades ago argued over which Midget player had made the key tackle. At the grocery store, a mother who'd never watched a football game in her life asked Cy when the next scrimmage was. Even the high school coach, who usually kept to himself, gave Cy a nod that meant more than words.

The town wasn't celebrating yet.

But it was paying attention.

The boys felt it too, though they didn't say it outright. It showed up in small ways — the way they carried themselves, the way they talked to each other, the way they replayed moments from the scrimmage like they were already memories worth keeping.

After practice one evening, a few of them lingered near the bleachers, sweaty and grass-stained, helmets dangling from their fingers.

Tony — helmet still crooked, chinstrap half snapped — nudged the safety who'd broken up the deep pass. "Man, that hit you made? I swear the whole field went quiet."

The safety shrugged, trying to play it off. "Just did what Coach said."

"Yeah," Tony said, grinning, "but you did it *fast*."

A couple of the linemen sat nearby, comparing bruises like badges of honor. One of them, a big kid who'd struggled with confidence last season, kept shaking his head.

"I can't believe we stopped 'em on that fourth down," he said. "Last year... I don't know if we would've."

His friend elbowed him. "Last year ain't this year."

Tom stood a little apart from the group, listening more than talking, but even he had a small smile tugging at the corner of his mouth. When one of the younger boys asked him how it felt to score the final touchdown, Tom just shrugged.

"Felt good," he said. "But it felt better that we all got there together."

The others nodded. They understood exactly what he meant.

Cy stood off to the side, pretending to check equipment but really just watching. The boys weren't bragging. They weren't getting cocky. They were just… proud. In the right way.

He saw something forming between them — trust, belief, a sense of belonging that couldn't be coached into existence. It had to be earned, moment by moment, rep by rep, hit by hit.

And they were earning it.

As the boys finally drifted toward their parents' cars, Cy felt the weight of the day settle in. Not heavy. Not burdensome.

Hopeful.

The kind of hope that made him think this season might be more than just games and practices.

TOM NOTICES SOMETHING NEW

After practice one night, while most of the boys were locked in on the upcoming league opener, Tom felt his thoughts drifting somewhere else entirely.

He'd noticed her before — during practice, on the far sideline with the cheer squad. She was a year younger, and her name was Chris. She wore her hair in a ponytail that bounced when she ran, and her voice carried when she called out chants. But it wasn't just that. It was something quieter. The way she focused. The way she smiled when she got a routine right. The way she didn't seem to notice anyone watching — especially not him.

But Tom was watching.

Not in a way he could explain. Not even to himself.

During the recent scrimmage, he caught glimpses of her between plays — standing with the other girls, clapping, cheering, laughing. And every time he did, something shifted in his chest. Not nerves. Not distraction.

Curiosity.

After practice the following week, he mentioned her — just barely — to one of his friends. A throwaway line. A half-mumbled observation.

"She's cool," he said, trying to sound casual.

His friend grinned. "You like her?"

Tom rolled his eyes. "No. I mean… I don't know."

That was all it took. The teasing started immediately — not cruel, just relentless. Elbows, smirks, exaggerated winks every time Chris walked by. Tom tried to brush it off, but it stuck to him like sweat after a long drill.

Then, one afternoon, a girl from his math class — someone who knew Chris — walked up to him near the bleachers.

"She asked if I thought you liked her," Jenna said, smiling.

Tom blinked. "What'd you tell her?"

"I said you might," she said. "And that you're not bad once you stop mumbling."

Tom laughed, embarrassed but grateful.

From that moment on, something began to shift. Not fast. Not dramatic. Just a quiet awareness between two kids trying to figure out what growing up felt like. Chris smiled a little longer when she saw him. Tom stood a little taller when she was nearby. Neither of them said much. But they didn't have to.

Over time, Jenna's words stayed with Tom.

He didn't know what to do with any of it. He didn't tell his friends — not after the teasing he'd already endured — but the thought kept sneaking up on him during drills, in the locker room, even while he lay in bed at night staring at the ceiling.

By Friday, he'd convinced himself it didn't mean anything. Girls talked. Maybe Jenna was just stirring the pot.

But then came Saturday.

Tom and a group of teammates ended up at Gino's Pizza, the unofficial hangout spot for every kid in Galesburg. The place was loud, crowded, and smelled like melted cheese and oregano. The boys grabbed a booth near the back, shoving and laughing as they argued over who had blown the biggest block in practice that morning.

Tom was halfway through a slice and some iced tea when the door jingled.

He didn't look up at first — not until Marcus elbowed him.

"Dude," Marcus whispered, "cheer squad at three o'clock."

Tom's stomach tightened. He glanced over.

There she was.

Chris walked in with three other girls, all of them talking at once, ponytails bouncing, jackets half-zipped. She looked different out of uniform — more relaxed, more like the girl he saw in the hallways at school. She scanned the room, laughing at something one of her friends said.

Then her eyes landed on him.

It wasn't dramatic. No movie moment. Just a flicker of recognition — a small, surprised smile that warmed her whole face.

Tom felt his ears heat up.

Marcus grinned. "Oh yeah. She definitely knows you."

"Shut up," Tom muttered, but he couldn't stop smiling.

The girls took a table near the jukebox. For a few minutes, Tom pretended to focus on his friends' conversation, but his attention kept drifting. Every so often, he caught Chris glancing his way. Not staring — just checking. Curious.

Finally, as Tom got up to get another iced tea, their paths crossed.

Literally.

He turned from the counter just as she stepped up beside him. They nearly bumped into each other.

"Oh — sorry," Tom said quickly.

Chris laughed softly. "It's okay. I wasn't looking."

There was a pause — not awkward, just… new.

"You guys played really well last week," she said. "The scrimmage. It was fun to watch."

Tom shrugged, trying to play it cool. "Yeah, it was… it was a good game."

"You scored, right?"

"Yeah. End of the fourth."

"I thought so." She smiled again, a little shy this time. "You looked really focused."

Tom swallowed. "You… uh… you looked like you were having fun cheering."

She laughed. "I was. I still mess up some of the routines, but I'm getting better."

Another pause. This one lingered.

Then Chris said, "Jenna told me she talked to you."

Tom's heart jumped. "She… she talks a lot."

"She does," Chris agreed, smiling. "But I'm glad she did."

He didn't know what to say to that. His brain scrambled for something clever, something smooth, something that didn't make him sound like a complete idiot.

What came out was: "Cool."

Chris laughed — not at him, but in a way that made him feel lighter.

"Well," she said, stepping aside so he could pass, "maybe I'll see you after the game next week."

"Yeah," Tom said. "Definitely."

As he walked back to the table, Marcus was already smirking.

"You were gone a while," he said. "Everything okay?"

Tom tried to hide the grin tugging at his mouth. "Yeah. Everything's fine."

But inside, something had shifted — small, quiet, but real.

The kind of shift that sticks with a fifteen-year-old boy long after the pizza's gone cold.

SIGNALS ON AND OFF THE FIELD

The first league game arrived with the kind of anticipation only small towns can generate. Posters hung in shop windows. Parents rearranged work schedules. The field was freshly lined, the bleachers scrubbed down, and the concession stand smelled like something special.

That smell? Pasta fazool.

Every home game, one of the players' moms — Mrs. DiAngelo — made a giant tub of it from an old

Italian recipe passed down through her family. It simmered all morning in the back of the concession stand, ladled out in Styrofoam cups to anyone lucky enough to get there before it ran out. It wasn't just food. It was tradition. It was comfort. It was Galesburg.

Joanne had added another layer to the game-day experience. She'd organized printed programs — black-and-white pages with team photos, player names, and short bios. Inside were shout-outs to the league's sponsors: Joe's Wine Store, Amity Used Cars, Wagner Carpet, and the rest. The programs sold for a few bucks each, and every dollar went back into the league. It was her idea — simple, smart, and effective.

"People want something to hold," she'd said. "Something to take home. Let's give it to them."

The Ponies played first.

They came out sharp — fast, disciplined, and hungry. Stosh had them ready, and for most of the game they traded blows with a tough visiting squad. The crowd leaned in with every snap, the cheer squad's voices rising and falling with the momentum.

Late in the fourth, the Ponies trailed by three but were driving. A crisp slant brought them into scoring range, and the bleachers roared. But on the next play, a misread led to an interception that sealed the game.

The Ponies lost 17–14.

It stung, but the applause afterward was real. The town saw something in those boys — grit, promise, a spark worth believing in.

Tom watched from the sideline with the rest of the Midgets, helmet in hand. He felt for them. He knew how close games like that could cut.

Chris was cheering that game, and when the Ponies walked off the field, she caught Tom's eye and gave him a small, encouraging smile — not for the Ponies, but for him.

He nodded back, trying not to look like it meant as much as it did.

Marcus noticed anyway. "Dude," he whispered, "you're in trouble."

Tom shoved him lightly. "Shut up."

But he was smiling.

Then it was Tom's turn.

The Midgets took the field with confidence — maybe too much of it. Cy had warned them all week not to underestimate the opener, but the boys came out blazing: two quick touchdowns, a dominant defensive stand, and a swagger that bordered on dangerous.

By halftime, they were up 21–0.

And that's when it started to slip.

They got sloppy. Missed blocks. Lazy tackles. A fumble on a handoff they'd run a hundred times. The other team clawed back, one score at a time. By the middle of the fourth, it was 21–18, and the Midgets looked stunned.

Cy didn't yell. He didn't panic. He just stood with his arms crossed, watching.

Finally, with two minutes left, the Midgets forced a fumble and recovered it. They ran out the clock and escaped with the win.

Relief washed over the sideline, and Cy gathered them quickly.

"You don't let your guard down," he said. "Not ever. You play hard until the last whistle. That's the difference between good and great."

The boys nodded, chastened.

They'd won — but they'd learned something more important.

After the game, the players mingled near the bleachers. Tom stood with Marcus, sipping a soda, replaying the sloppy second half in his head.

Chris walked by with her squad, laughing with friends. She paused when she saw him.

"You played great," she said.

Tom shrugged. "We almost blew it."

"Yeah," she said, smiling, "but you didn't."

They stood there for a moment — not long, not awkward. Just enough.

Then she rejoined her friends, and Tom watched her go.

Marcus elbowed him. "You gonna talk to her for real sometime?"

Tom didn't answer.

Tuesday's practice had a different feel to it. The excitement of opening weekend had faded, replaced by the sting of mistakes and the weight of expectations.

Dwyer and Stosh ran a tight session — no yelling, no theatrics, just honest evaluation.

The Ponies worked on red-zone timing, replaying the final drive from Saturday until the routes were crisp and the reads were clean. Stosh kept reminding them, "One play doesn't define you. How you respond does."

On the other side of the field, the Midgets ran pursuit drills and ball-security circuits. Cy made them redo a fumbled exchange from the game until it was second nature again. The boys were tired, humbled, and focused.

Tom felt it more than most.

He'd played well, but he knew the team had let their guard down. And he hated that feeling — the sense that they'd almost handed the game away. He ran drills with a quiet intensity, pushing himself harder than usual.

During water break, Marcus wandered over, smirking like he'd been waiting for the right moment.

"So," he said, "you and Chris, huh?"

Tom groaned. "Not this again."

Marcus nudged him. "Dude, she talked to you after the game. She smiled. She STOPPED WALKING to talk to you. That means something."

"Can you not make a big deal out of it?" Tom said, though his face was already warming.

Marcus grinned wider. "It IS a big deal."

Tom tried to brush it off, but the teasing stuck with him. Not in a bad way — more like pressure he didn't know how to handle. He liked Chris. He knew that now. And the more Marcus pushed, the more Tom realized he didn't want to keep pretending otherwise.

By Wednesday, the pressure had turned into something else — determination.

Tom spotted Chris at her locker before first period. She was talking with a friend, books tucked under her arm, ponytail bouncing as she laughed at something the other girl said.

Tom's heart thumped hard enough to feel in his throat.

Just go, he told himself.

He walked up before he could talk himself out of it.

"Hey," he said, trying to sound casual.

Chris turned, surprised but smiling. "Hey, Tom."

For a second, neither of them spoke. Then Tom cleared his throat.

"I, uh… wanted to say thanks. For what you said after the game."

She shrugged lightly. "You played great. I meant it."

Tom nodded, feeling braver than he expected. "Maybe… maybe we could talk sometime? Like… not just at games."

Chris's smile widened — warm, genuine, a little shy. "I'd like that."

She pulled a pen from her binder, tore a small corner from a notebook page, and scribbled something down. Then she handed it to him.

Her phone number.

Tom stared at it for a second, stunned that something so small could feel so huge.

"Call me tonight," she said, then headed off to class with her friend.

Tom stood there a moment longer, the paper warm in his hand.

That night, after pacing his room for a good ten minutes, Tom finally called her.

They talked about school. About the game. About music. About nothing and everything. The conversation stretched longer than he expected, easy and natural in a way that made him feel lighter.

By the time he finally put his phone down, he realized something:

Football wasn't the only thing on his mind anymore.

And he didn't mind that at all.

RISE OF THE RAIDERS

Week Two arrived with a different kind of energy — not nervous, not jittery, but hungry. The Ponies boarded the bus early Saturday morning, shoulder pads clacking, helmets tucked under their arms, the smell of fresh-cut grass still clinging to their uniforms from Friday's walkthrough. Stosh moved up and down the aisle, tapping helmets, offering quick reminders.

"Stay disciplined." "Trust your reads." "Play your game."

The boys nodded, eyes forward. They wanted this one.

The field in East Valley wasn't much to look at — patchy grass, crooked goalposts, a scoreboard that flickered every time someone ran the concession-stand popcorn popper. But the Ponies didn't care. They came out sharp, moving the ball with confidence. Their quarterback hit a deep out route early, and the sideline erupted. The defense swarmed, tackling with purpose.

By halftime, they led 7–3.

The fourth quarter was a grind — East Valley pounding the ball, Galesburg bending but refusing to break. With two minutes left, the Ponies forced a fumble near midfield. Stosh pumped his fist. The boys ran out the clock, sealing a 14–10 win.

Parents hugged. Players shouted. Even the bus ride home felt different — louder, prouder, like they'd finally stepped into the league instead of just visiting it.

Tom watched from the Midget sideline that day, proud of the younger squad.

"They earned that," he said to Marcus.

Marcus nodded. "About time people stop sleeping on Galesburg."

The Midgets' game that afternoon was a mud-splattered slugfest. The field was soft, cleats sinking with every step. Tom's socks were soaked by the end of warmups. Cy didn't care.

"Conditions don't matter," he said. "Execution does."

The game stayed tight. Tom caught a touchdown on a rollout, slipping in the mud but keeping his balance long enough to reach the end zone. The defense held strong, but the other team kept pushing. With four minutes left, Galesburg led 21–14.

That's when Cy called Tony Matz's number.

Tony jogged onto the field, eyes wide, breathing fast. Tom slapped his shoulder pad. "You got this."

On Tony's second play, the other team ran a sweep to his side. Tony hesitated — just a heartbeat — and the runner burst past him for a thirty-yard gain. The sideline groaned. Cy made the substitution quietly.

Tony stood alone near the bench, helmet dangling from his fingers.

Tom walked over, calm and steady. "You saw it late. Happens."

Tony didn't look up. "I cost us the game."

"No," Tom said. "You missed one play. Big difference."

Tony swallowed hard. "Coach won't trust me again."

Tom shook his head. "He will. But you gotta trust yourself first."

Tony finally met his eyes. "You really think so?"

"I know so."

Cy watched the exchange from the sideline, arms crossed, expression unreadable. But inside, he felt something shift. Leadership wasn't something you coached into a kid. It showed up when it mattered.

The Midgets held on to win 21–17.

The next week brought two more road games.

The Ponies fought tooth and nail in a tough matchup against a team known for speed. They led late, but a fumble and a missed tackle turned the tide. They lost 21–17, but the coaches saw something important — they weren't getting pushed around anymore.

"They're legit," Stosh said afterward. "We're legit."

The Midgets, meanwhile, faced a team that chirped during warmups. Cy ignored it.

"Talk doesn't win games," he said.

Tom played one of his best games — poised, patient, reading the defense like he'd been doing it for years.

It started in Week Two warmups. Tom ran a deep post route during pregame, leaping high over a defender to snag a ball with one hand — twisting midair, landing light on his feet, and turning upfield in one fluid motion.

Marcus whistled. "Dude… that looked like Lynn Swann," referring to Lynn Swann, the standout wide receiver for the Pittsburgh Steelers.

Coach Dwyer overheard. "Swann wears eighty-eight too," he said, nodding at Tom's jersey. "Maybe we got our own Swanny."

The name stuck instantly.

By kickoff, half the Midgets were calling him that.

Tom pretended to hate it.

He didn't.

The offensive line held strong and the defense swarmed. They won 28–20, improving to 3–0.

By the time the bus rolled back into Galesburg, the whispers had started.

"Undefeated." "Best team in the league?" "Maybe this is their year."

Tuesday's practice felt electric.

The Ponies ran red-zone drills with crisp execution. Stosh barked corrections but with pride in his voice.

"You're not the same team you were three weeks ago. Keep climbing."

The Midgets worked on pursuit angles, ball security, and situational awareness. Cy pulled Tony aside during warmups.

"You're getting another shot," he said. "Be ready."

Tony nodded, jaw set.

Tom overheard and smiled. "Told you."

During water break, Marcus nudged Tom. "So… you and Chris. Still calling her?"

Tom rolled his eyes. "Yeah."

Marcus grinned. "You gonna ask her out or just pretend she's one of the guys?"

Tom shoved him lightly. "Shut up."

But he was smiling.

That night, Cy and Tom rode home from practice in comfortable silence. The windows were down, the air warm and soft. Tom stared out at the passing trees, thinking about the next game, about Tony, about Chris.

Cy glanced over.

"So," he said, "you and the cheerleader."

Tom blinked. "What?"

"Chris, isn't it?" Cy said. "I saw you two talking after the game."

Tom hesitated. "We've been talking."

Cy nodded. "She seems nice."

"She is."

Another pause.

"You're fifteen," Cy said. "Things start to shift around now. You notice girls. They notice you. It's normal."

Tom didn't answer.

Cy smiled faintly. "Just remember — you're still you. Football, school, friends. That stuff doesn't go away. You just learn how to carry more."

Tom nodded. "I like her."

"I know," Cy said. "Just take your time. Be honest. And don't forget who you are."

Tom looked out the window again, but this time he was smiling.

Week Four arrived with a sense of momentum Galesburg hadn't felt in years. It was the third road game in as many weeks, and the town was buzzing — not just about the Midgets' undefeated run, but about the Ponies proving they belonged too. Kids wore their jerseys to school. Parents talked about the standings at the grocery store. Even teachers asked how the teams were doing.

And everywhere Tom went, someone called him "Swanny."

At first it embarrassed him. Then it motivated him. Now, it was becoming something else entirely.

A standard.

Week Four saw the Ponies start the game with a quiet confidence that hadn't been there before. They faced a team known for speed but light on discipline. From the opening kickoff, the Ponies controlled the tempo, scoring on a sixty-yard run on the second play of the game. The defense held firm, swarming the edges and forcing turnovers.

By halftime, the Ponies led 20–6, and they never looked back. Stosh rotated players in the fourth quarter, letting the younger kids get reps while the starters cheered from the sideline.

Final score: Ponies 26, Chargers 12.

A clean, confident win — the kind that made the long bus ride home feel like a celebration.

The Week Four Midgets opponent was different. Bigger. Faster. Meaner. They were the kind of team that warmed up like they were preparing for war — slamming pads, barking at each other, staring down the Raiders from across the field.

Cy gathered his boys before kickoff.

"They're good," he said. "But so are we. Play your game. Trust each other. And don't let anyone take your confidence."

Tom felt the words settle into him. He tugged at his #88 jersey, rolled his shoulders, and looked across the field. The other team's corners were tall and physical.

The game opened with a punch.

On the first play from scrimmage, Tom ran a deep comeback route. The corner tried to jam him, but

Tom slipped past, planted hard, and came back to the ball. The catch was clean, the crowd roared, and Marcus shouted from the sideline:

"Swanny's here!"

But the other team answered quickly. Their running back was a tank, breaking tackles and dragging defenders. By halftime, the score was tied 14–14.

The Midgets had never been punched in the mouth like this so far this season.

And they didn't like it.

Midway through the third quarter, the game shifted.

"Matz! Get in there!"

Tony froze for half a second, then sprinted onto the field. Tom slapped his shoulder pad as he passed.

"You got this," Tom said. "Go get it."

The ball snapped. The running back took the pitch and sprinted toward the edge — a toss sweep, the same play Tony had missed two weeks earlier.

Tony read it instantly.

He didn't hesitate.

He didn't think.

He attacked.

He shot through the gap, wrapped the runner's legs, and drove him into the turf. The sideline exploded. Cy pumped his fist once — a rare show of emotion.

Tom was the first to reach him.

"That's how you do it!" he shouted, grabbing Tony's helmet. "That's how you respond!"

Tony's eyes were wide, breath shaking. "I... I got him."

"You didn't just get him," Tom said. "You changed the game."

And he had.

The Midgets fed off the energy of seeing Tony redeem himself. Anything felt possible. Everything. The defense tightened. The offense found rhythm. Tom made two clutch catches on the next drive — one a leaping grab over the middle, the other a toe-tap on the sideline that had parents gasping.

"Swanny!" the crowd chanted.

For the first time, Tom didn't pretend not to hear it.

He embraced it.

After the game — a 28–24 win that left everyone exhausted and exhilarated — the players mingled near the buses. Tom was still buzzing from the adrenaline when he saw Chris walking toward him, ponytail bouncing, Raiders cheer jacket zipped halfway up.

"You were amazing today," she said, smiling.

Tom shrugged, trying to play it cool. "Team effort."

She rolled her eyes. "You can say you played well, you know."

He laughed. "Okay. I played well."

She stepped a little closer. "I like watching you play."

Tom felt his chest tighten — not in a bad way, but in the way that made him suddenly aware of everything: the cool air, the noise of teammates behind him, the way Chris's eyes held his for a second longer than usual.

"You wanna… maybe hang out sometime?" he asked.

Chris smiled. "I'd like that."

It wasn't dramatic. It wasn't a movie moment.

It was real.

And it was enough.

On the ride home, Cy kept glancing at Tom in his seat. Tom was staring out the window, smiling at nothing.

"You played a hell of a game," Cy said.

Tom nodded. "Thanks."

"And Tony… that was big."

"Yeah," Tom said. "He earned it."

Cy paused. "You helped him earn it. That's what leaders do."

Tom didn't respond, but the smile stayed.

After a moment, Cy added, "And Chris seems like a nice girl."

Tom's ears went red. "Dad…"

Cy chuckled. "Hey, I'm not giving you a hard time. Just saying… I see you growing up. On the field and off."

Tom looked out the window again, but this time the smile was different.

Quieter.

Prouder.

By Monday morning, the school hallways were buzzing.

"Did you see Swanny's catch?" "Dude, he mossed that kid." "Tony Matz is a beast now." "The Midgets are undefeated!"

Tom walked to class with his backpack slung over one shoulder, trying not to look like he was listening. But he heard every word.

And for the first time, he felt like he wasn't just part of the team.

He was part of something bigger.

Something rising.

Four weeks in, sitting at 4–0 with two straight home games ahead, the momentum felt real. For the first time all season, Tom let himself breathe.

Life was good.

THE MIDGETS TRAP GAME

Galesburg was glowing. Unlike the previous year at this point in the season, both the Ponies and the Midgets had earned something new: league respect. Posters filled shop windows. Local businesses ran game-day specials. A Friday night pep rally drew more people than the last school fundraiser.

And everywhere you looked, someone was talking football.

Tom Mozatta was talking too — but mostly about himself.

The nickname had taken on a life of its own.

"Swanny!" echoed from the bleachers every time Tom caught a pass. Kids wrote **#88** on homemade signs. Even the local paper ran a photo of his Week Four touchdown with the caption:

MOZATTA SOARS AGAIN

Tom liked it.

Maybe too much.

He walked into school that Monday with his Raiders hoodie zipped halfway down, nodding at classmates like he was floating above the hallway. Chris met him at his locker, smiling, and Tom felt like the whole world was tilting in his favor.

They'd been talking almost every night. She'd started calling him "Swanny" too — half teasing, half proud.

By game day, Tom wasn't just confident.

He was cocky.

Joanne's printed programs for Week Five sold out before kickoff.

Two giant pots of pasta fazool simmered in the concession stand, filling the air with the smell of garlic and tomatoes.

The Ponies played first — a home game against a struggling team that never found its footing. Stosh's boys came out sharp, scoring early and often. The defense swarmed. The offense clicked. They won 35–7, and the crowd loved every second.

Tom watched from the Midget sideline, arms crossed, smiling.

"They're rolling," Marcus said.

Tom nodded. "We're next."

The Midgets' opponent had only one loss, but all their wins were close. Everyone expected a Galesburg victory — the town, the coaches, the players.

And Tom.

He jogged out for warmups with his chin high, scanning the field until he spotted Chris in her cheer uniform, laughing with her squad. She waved. He waved back.

Cy watched from the sideline, arms crossed.

He didn't like the looseness. The jokes. The half-speed drills.

He pulled them in before kickoff.

"Respect every opponent," he said. "Every snap. Every quarter. Every game."

Tom nodded, but his eyes drifted back to Chris.

The Midgets scored early — a quick drive capped by a short run from Marcus. 6–0.

But after that, things got strange.

Tom dropped a pass he normally caught in his sleep. The defense missed assignments. The offense stalled. The other team, scrappy and determined, hung around.

By the fourth quarter, it was still 6–0.

Cy paced the sideline, jaw tight.

The Midgets lined up on defense with just under four minutes left, barely clinging to a lead that should have been bigger. The crowd was restless, sensing something was off. Cy felt it too — the looseness, the drifting focus, the way the boys kept glancing at the scoreboard like the game was already over.

And Tom… Tom was the loosest of all.

Breaking huddle, he jogged to his spot at cornerback, tapping his helmet as the crowd chanted "Swanny!" from the bleachers. He loved it. He soaked it in. He even gave a little wave — something he'd never done before.

Then he looked toward the cheer line.

Chris was there, smiling, bouncing with the rhythm of the chant. She caught his eye and gave him a small, excited nod.

Tom's chest swelled.

He wasn't just playing well.

He was **the guy**.

He turned back toward the offense, but the image of Chris lingered like an afterimage burned into his vision.

The opposing offense broke the huddle and came out in a heavy I formation — two tight ends, fullback, tailback. Classic power run look. The kind of formation that screamed **WE'RE COMING RIGHT AT YOU**.

Tom shifted forward, ready to crash the edge.

His assignment was simple: **man coverage on #82**, their only real receiving threat. Stay with him. Don't get caught peeking.

But Tom wasn't thinking about #82.

He was thinking about Chris.

And the nickname.

And the crowd.

And how good it felt to be undefeated.

The quarterback barked the cadence.

"Set… hut!"

The ball snapped. The fullback and tailback surged right, selling the sweep. The offensive line flowed that direction too, helmets shifting like a wave.

Tom bit hard.

Too hard.

He took two aggressive steps toward the backfield, eyes locked on the running back — the same kid who had gashed them earlier in the quarter.

He never saw #82 slip behind him.

The running back sprinted toward the sideline, then suddenly slowed, pivoted, and cocked his arm back.

A halfback pass.

The oldest trick in the book.

Tom's stomach dropped.

He spun around, cleats digging into the turf, but it was too late. #82 was already five yards behind him, running free down the sideline.

Tom pumped his arms, sprinting as hard as he could, but the separation was too great. The crowd gasped — a sharp, collective inhale — as the ball arced through the air in a perfect spiral.

Time slowed.

Tom reached out, fingertips brushing nothing but wind.

The ball dropped into #82's hands like it belonged there.

Touchdown.

The stadium went silent except for the visiting sideline erupting in cheers.

Tom stood in the end zone, hands on his hips, chest heaving. He stared at the grass, replaying the moment — the fake, the bite, the turn, the helpless chase.

He knew exactly what he'd done.

He'd abandoned his assignment.

He'd let his ego take the wheel.

He'd let the crowd — and Chris — pull his focus away from the game.

The extra point clanked off the upright.

6–6.

A tie.

A game they were supposed to win.

A game they nearly lost because of him.

When the final whistle blew, the Midgets trudged toward the sideline. No cheers. No high fives. Just quiet.

Tom sat on the bench, helmet dangling from his fingers, staring at the field like it had betrayed him.

Marcus approached. "Tough play, man."

Tom didn't look up. "I blew it."

Cy walked over slowly, crouched in front of him.

"You weren't focused," Cy said. "You were watching her."

Tom's throat tightened. "I know."

"You're a leader on this team," Cy said. "Leaders don't get distracted."

Tom swallowed hard. "I thought… I thought I had everything under control."

Cy shook his head gently. "That's when football humbles you. When life humbles you."

Tom nodded, eyes burning.

He didn't feel like Swanny anymore.

He felt like a kid who'd let everyone down — his team, his coaches, his dad, and himself.

And he didn't know how to fix it.

Not yet.

The tie hit Galesburg harder than anyone expected.

A 6–6 final against a team they were supposed to beat at home felt like a loss. The crowd filed out quietly, murmuring in small clusters. Parents shook their heads. Younger kids kicked at gravel. Even the cheer squad seemed unsure how to react.

The Midgets walked toward the locker room in a slow, uneven line — helmets loose, pads unstrapped, eyes down.

Tom walked in the middle of them, feeling every stare.

He didn't need anyone to tell him what happened.

He knew.

Inside the locker room, the air was thick and heavy. No one spoke at first. Shoulder pads clattered to the floor. Cleats scraped against concrete. The usual postgame chatter was gone.

Marcus finally broke the silence.

"We should've had them."

A few players nodded.

Another kid added, "We got sloppy."

Someone else said, "We weren't focused."

Tom waited for someone to say it.

To say **his** mistake.

But no one did.

They didn't have to.

He could feel it in the way they avoided his eyes. In the way conversations shifted when he walked by. In the way the room tilted away from him.

He sat on the bench, elbows on his knees, helmet dangling between his hands.

He didn't feel like Swanny.

He felt like a fraud.

By Monday morning, the whispers had started.

At the gas station: "Should've been a win." At the diner: "Something's off with the Midgets." At school: "Did you see that trick play? He got smoked."

Tom heard it all.

He kept his head down in the hallways, hoodie pulled tight, backpack slung low. The confidence he'd carried last week — the swagger, the nickname, the attention — evaporated.

He didn't even want to look at Chris.

But she found him anyway.

She caught up to him at his locker, ponytail swaying, expression soft.

"Hey," she said.

Tom didn't look up. "Hey."

"You okay?"

He shrugged. "Not really."

She leaned against the locker next to his. "You know… one bad play doesn't erase everything else you've done."

"It wasn't just a bad play," Tom said. "It cost us the game."

"It cost you a win," she corrected. "Not the season."

He finally looked at her.

"You're allowed to mess up," she said. "You're human. Even if everyone else forgets that sometimes."

Tom swallowed. "I just… I let everyone down."

Chris shook her head. "You didn't let me down."

Something in his chest loosened — not fixed, but less tight.

Later that day, Tony found him sitting alone on a bench outside school, staring at the trees.

"You know," Tony said, dropping his backpack beside him, "you're the reason I didn't quit."

Tom blinked. "What?"

"When I missed that tackle in Week Two," Tony said, "I thought I was done. But you came over. You talked to me. You made me believe I could get better."

Tom looked away. "That's different."

"No," Tony said firmly. "It's not."

He nudged Tom's shoulder. "You messed up. So what? Fix it. That's what you told me."

Tom let out a slow breath. "I don't know if I can."

Tony smirked. "Then I guess I'll have to remind you every day until you do."

Tom laughed — small, tired, but real.

Cy didn't yell at practice that week.

He didn't need to.

He ran them hard — crisp routes, clean footwork, perfect reads. Every drill had purpose. Every mistake was corrected immediately. Every rep mattered.

Tom felt something shift inside him.

He wasn't thinking about the crowd. He wasn't thinking about the nickname. He wasn't thinking about Chris.

He was thinking about football.

About doing his job.

About earning respect, not assuming it.

During a one-on-one drill, he ran a deep out route so sharp the corner fell trying to keep up. The ball hit him in stride. The team erupted.

Marcus shouted, "There he is! That's Swanny!"

But this time, Tom didn't wave.

He didn't smile.

He just jogged back to the huddle, focused, breathing steady.

He wasn't chasing the nickname anymore.

He was earning it.

A DIFFERENT KIND OF WIN

The tie still lingered. All week, the Midgets practiced harder. Quieter. No jokes on the field. Cy didn't yell. He didn't need to. The disappointment was enough.

Week Six at home proved too tough for the Ponies, who fell 24–20 to a solid team.

The Midgets' opponent brought speed — not size, not power, but pure speed. Jet sweeps, bubble screens, quick slants. Their quarterback was small but slippery, and their corners played press coverage like they had something to prove.

Cy gathered the boys before kickoff.

"They're fast," he said. "So we play smart. We play clean. We play together."

Tom nodded, helmet tucked under his arm.

He wasn't thinking about the crowd. He wasn't thinking about Chris. He was thinking about his assignment.

The Midgets opened with a long drive — twelve plays, seventy yards, capped by a short run from Marcus. No celebration. No dancing. Just a quiet jog back to the sideline.

Tom caught two passes on the drive — one a comeback route, the other a slant he turned upfield for a first down. Both were clean. Both were disciplined.

"Nice work," Cy said as he passed.

Tom nodded. "Just doing my job."

The other team tried to stretch the field — quick passes, motion, misdirection. But the Midgets stayed home. Tony made a key tackle on third down, reading the play before it developed.

Tom lined up at cornerback, eyes locked on his receiver. No peeking. No drifting. No distractions.

On one play, the quarterback pump-faked a screen and launched a deep ball. Tom stayed with his man, turned at the right moment, and knocked it away.

The sideline erupted.

"Swanny!" someone shouted.

Tom didn't react.

He just jogged back to the huddle.

The Midgets led 14–0 at the break.

Cy didn't give a speech.

He just said, "Keep earning it."

Tom knelt on the grass, sucking on a fresh orange slice, staring at the field.

Chris walked past with her squad and gave him a small wave.

He nodded back — quick, respectful, focused.

She smiled.

That was enough.

The third quarter was a grind — no big plays, no highlight reels. Just solid football. The offensive line held strong. The defense swarmed. Tom made a key third-down catch in traffic, absorbing a hit and popping right back up.

Cy clapped once.

Tom nodded.

No flash.

Just football.

The Midgets won 21–7.

No blowout. No collapse. Just discipline.

Earned.

Tom sat on the bench afterward, helmet off, breathing steady.

Marcus walked over. "You're back."

Tom smiled. "I never left. I just got distracted."

Tony grinned. "You're Swanny again."

The rest of the Midgets drifted in around him — not in a rush, not in a crowd, but in that quiet, respectful way teammates do when they've seen something shift. A couple of linemen bumped his shoulder pads. Eddie

Fisher gave him a nod that meant more than words. Even Coach Dwyer, who never praised in the moment, let his hand rest on Tom's back for half a second before moving on.

Word traveled fast in Galesburg. By the time the boys reached the parking lot, a few parents were already talking.

"Tom looked like himself again." "Good to see that kid focused." "Maybe the Midgets aren't done yet."

Tom heard it all, but it didn't swell his head this time.

It just settled him.

Chris walked beside him, hands in her jacket pockets.

"You played like you meant it today," she said — not teasing, not pushing, just noticing.

Tom felt the warmth of that. "I did."

"And you didn't try to do everything yourself."

"That too."

Tony jogged up, helmet and shoulder pads in hand. "Hey, Swanny — you hungry? Let's get cleaned up and head out for some pizza."

Tom laughed. "I could eat."

Chris added, "I'll come too. Someone has to make sure you two don't inhale the whole pie."

It wasn't a dramatic moment. Just three kids walking together with the late-afternoon sun catching the dust in the air, the weight of that tie fading behind them and their friendship ahead of them.

The pizza place was buzzing the way it always did after a Midgets game — families squeezed into booths, kids still wearing their jerseys, the smell of melted cheese drifting through the air. A couple of parents congratulated Tom as they walked in, but he didn't puff up or shrink away. He just nodded, steady and sure.

They found a booth near the back, the kind with cracked red vinyl seats. Tony grabbed the menu like he was preparing for battle. Chris slid in across from Tom, her smile easy, her eyes bright in the warm light.

Conversation started simple — the game, school, who had tripped over the kicking tee during warmups — but gradually, without anyone forcing it, Tom and Chris drifted into their own rhythm.

She asked about the route he ran in the second quarter. He asked how her art project was coming along. She teased him about the way he celebrated after the touchdown. He pretended he didn't remember doing it.

Tony watched them for a while, grinning to himself. He wasn't annoyed. He wasn't left out. He just understood. Tom was a friend, and something good was happening. Something new.

Halfway through the pizza, Tony wiped his hands on a napkin and stood.

"Alright, I'm tapping out. I'm gonna head home before my mom thinks I got lost in the arcade."

Tom blinked. "You sure? We can—"

Tony cut him off with a smirk. "You two are fine. I'll see you tomorrow."

He gave Tom a quick high-five, waved at Chris, and slipped out the door, leaving the booth suddenly quieter, softer.

Tom and Chris stayed.

They talked until the dinner rush thinned and the clatter of dishes faded. When they finally stepped outside, the sky had shifted to a deep, dark blue, the streetlights humming to life.

"I can walk you home," Tom said, trying to sound casual.

Chris nodded. "I'd like that."

They walked side by side, their steps falling into the same rhythm. The night air was cool, carrying the faint smell of cut grass and someone's backyard grill. Tom felt calm — not distracted, not nervous — just present.

"You played really well today," Chris said. "Like… really well."

Tom shrugged, but he couldn't hide the small smile. "I felt like myself again."

"You looked like yourself," she said. "Focused. Confident."

They reached her house, the porch light glowing softly. She turned toward him, hands tucked into her sleeves, eyes warm.

"I had fun tonight," she said.

"Me too."

A quiet moment settled between them — not awkward, not rushed. Just full.

Tom leaned in, slow enough that she could step back if she wanted.

She didn't.

Their first kiss was soft and brief, but it carried a weight neither of them would forget. It wasn't fireworks. It wasn't dramatic.

It was real.

When they pulled apart, Chris looked down, smiling in a way that made Tom's chest feel too small for his heart.

"Goodnight, Tom."

"Goodnight."

She slipped inside, and Tom stood there for a moment, letting the night settle around him. Then he turned and started home, hands in his pockets, steps light.

Tom didn't feel pulled in two directions anymore.

He felt anchored.

Football mattered. Chris mattered.

And instead of competing for space in his head, they steadied him.

That kiss didn't magically make him a better player. But it made him want to be one.

It made him want to finish the season strong — for his team, for his dad, for himself… and for the girl who believed in him even when he'd lost his way.

Swanny was back.

And now he knew exactly why.

The next practice came, and the Midgets trickled onto the field in small clusters, stretching, complaining about homework or chores.

Tom arrived quietly, helmet in hand, but something about him was different.

Not louder. Not cockier. Just… centered.

Tony noticed first. "Swanny, you look like you had a good night with Chris."

Tom shrugged, but the small smile gave him away. "Yeah. I did."

Tony jogged over, grinning. "Somebody's glowing."

Tom elbowed him. "Shut up."

Tony laughed. "I'm just saying. You look… I don't know. Balanced."

Chris wasn't at practice — but Tom felt her presence anyway, like a steady warmth in the back of his mind. Not a distraction. Not something pulling him away from football. More like something that helped him breathe.

Cy blew his whistle, calling everyone into warmups. Tom fell into line, movements crisp, focused. He hit every drill with purpose. His footwork was sharp. His routes were clean. His cuts were decisive.

Cy watched him for a long moment, arms crossed.

When Tom finished a route, Cy nodded once — the closest thing he ever gave to praise during practice.

"Good. Again."

Tom ran it again, faster this time, smoother. The ball hit his hands with a satisfying thump.

Marcus muttered to Eddie Fisher, "Swanny's locked in."

Eddie nodded. "Yep."

But it wasn't said with judgment.

It was said with relief — like the team had been waiting to make sure this version of Tom stayed.

During a water break, Tony leaned against the fence beside him.

"So… you walked her home?"

Tom didn't answer right away. He just took a sip of water, eyes on the field.

Tony grinned. "You did."

Tom finally nodded. "Yeah."

"And?"

Tom's smile was small, private, but unmistakable. "And… it was good."

Tony didn't tease him. Not this time. He just bumped his shoulder.

"Knew it."

The following weeks felt different for the Ponies. The next matchup brought the Coalton Heights Ironmen, a team known for grinding games down to dust. The Ponies hung tough but fell short late, losing by a touchdown. It stung — the kind of loss that sits in a kid's chest for a few days — but it didn't break them.

Weeks Eight, Nine, and Ten told a different story. They beat the Iron Hollow Miners with a balanced attack — their star running back pounding the ball inside, their developing quarterback hitting short passes that kept the chains moving, and a defense making open-field tackles that had parents cheering from the bleachers. They edged out the Forge Ridge Falcons in a defensive slugfest, the kind of game where every kid walked off the field covered in mud and pride. And in Week Ten, they stunned the Millstone Mustangs on the road, silencing a notoriously loud home crowd with a late fourth-quarter drive that showed just how far they'd come.

The Ponies weren't perfect. But they grew better each week. And the town saw it. Something had clicked — not just in the playbook, but in the boys themselves. They weren't the biggest team in the East Valley Intercity League, and they weren't the flashiest, but they learned how to fight for every yard, every tackle, every inch of progress.

Meanwhile, the Midgets kept rolling. Week after week, they found ways to win — sometimes with big plays, sometimes with grit, sometimes with pure stubbornness. But they never lost. Not once.

And behind it all, the Pee Wees kept practicing in the background — helmets too big, jerseys hanging loose, learning how to line up straight and how to fall without crying. Parents clapped for every small victory. Coaches knelt down to tie shoes and wipe noses. It was the quiet heartbeat of the league, the reminder that some of the Midgets and Ponies had once been one of them.

By the time the final whistle blew on Week Ten, **Galesburg had something real to hold onto.**

The Ponies finished 6–4, a winning record that felt earned, not given. The Midgets finished 9–0–1, an incredible season considering the league had nearly dropped them before it even began. And the Pee Wees?

They finished with smiles, a few boo-boos, and the promise of next year.

The Ponies' season ended with heads high. Their final record wasn't perfect, but it felt like a triumph. They had grown from a shaky, uncertain group into a team that fought for every yard and believed in each other. Their last win — a gritty road victory — sealed the feeling that they were on the rise. When the boys walked off the field that day, helmets tucked under their arms, they weren't disappointed the season was over.

They were proud of how far they'd come.

But for Galesburg, football wasn't done.

Not yet.

The East Valley Intercity League had a simple rule: the top two teams played for the championship on the biggest high school field in the region — East Valley High, with its towering bleachers, bright lights, and a press box that made even grown men feel small. The game would even be televised on local public access.

And because the league wanted the game to feel special, the teams got a full week off to prepare. No more regular-season games. No distractions. Just focus.

The Midgets were one of those two teams.

9–0–1. Undefeated. Unbroken. Unfinished.

There was something poetic — maybe even a little cruel — about the matchup the league served up. The Midgets would face the Alton Junction Railers, the only team they hadn't beaten. The tie in Week Five still hung in the air like unfinished business. It wasn't a loss, but it felt like one.

The Railers had turned out to be tougher than anyone expected — disciplined, physical, mistake-free. They finished 9–0–1 too.

As soon as the pairing was announced, the whole town felt a jolt of electricity. People talked about *revenge* without saying the word. They talked about *unfinished business* without needing to explain it. They talked about how the boys had grown since that game — steadier now, sharper, more connected.

The anticipation wasn't loud.

It simmered.

Parents whispered about it. Kids reenacted plays from the tie game at recess, insisting the Midgets would "get them this time." Even the Pee Wees felt it, admiring the older boys with wide eyes, sensing something big was coming.

Galesburg wasn't a place that made a big show of things, but pride seeped into everything. The diner on Main Street hung a banner that read **BRING IT HOME, RAIDERS!** The hardware store painted its windows blue and white. Even the old men outside the barbershop — the ones who never agreed on anything — nodded and said the boys had a real shot.

Galesburg wasn't just hoping for a championship.

They were hoping for closure.

For Tom, the news hit deeper than it did for anyone else.

He remembered Week Five too clearly — the trick play he bit on, the moment he drifted out of position, the split-second where he let his eyes wander instead of trusting his assignment. It wasn't the only reason the game ended in a tie, but it was *his* reason. And it had lived in the back of his mind ever since.

Now they were playing the Railers again. Under the biggest lights in East Valley. With the whole town watching.

Walking home after school one day, Tom felt the weight settle on his shoulders. Not crushing, but real. He wondered if he had it in him to let go of that mistake — to stop replaying it, stop fearing it, stop letting it define him. He wondered if he could still be the player he wanted to be, the one his teammates believed in, the one Chris saw when she looked at him.

He kicked a pebble down the sidewalk, hands in his pockets, thinking about his dad's words:

LEADERS DON'T GET DISTRACTED.

Maybe this game wasn't about erasing the mistake.

Maybe it was about proving he wasn't afraid of it.

Tom lifted his head, the cool night air filling his lungs. He didn't know what the championship would bring.

But he knew one thing:

He wasn't the kid from Week Five anymore.

And he was ready to show it.

For the Midgets, the week off wasn't a vacation.

It was a slow burn.

Practice felt sharper, more focused. Every drill had weight. Every rep mattered. The boys weren't nervous — not exactly — but they felt the size of what was coming. Playing at East Valley High was like stepping onto a college field. The turf was perfect. The lights were blinding. The stands seemed to stretch forever.

Tom felt it most of all.

He wasn't the loudest kid on the team, but he carried himself differently now — steady, grounded, confident in a way that came from more than football. The kiss with Chris, the talk with his dad, the way the season had unfolded… it all settled into him like a foundation he didn't know he'd been building.

Tony buzzed with energy, bouncing between excitement and nerves. Marcus kept things light, cracking jokes during warmups. Eddie Fisher was all business, his focus unshakeable. Every kid had his own way of handling the moment, but they all shared the same fire.

They wanted this. Not for glory. Not for bragging rights.

But because they had earned the chance to play for something bigger than themselves.

Cy and Dwyer felt the weight too, though they hid it well.

Coach Dwyer ran practices with a calm intensity, never raising his voice, never letting the boys get sloppy. He knew the championship wasn't about trick plays or fancy schemes. It was about discipline. Heart. Execution. The things he'd been drilling into them since August. But even he softened a little that week, clapping shoulders, offering quiet words of encouragement.

They weren't just coaching a team.

They were guiding a group of boys through a moment they'd remember for the rest of their lives.

Parents felt a mix of pride and nerves. They packed blankets, hand warmers, and thermoses for the big game. They talked about carpools, rally signs, parking, and whether East Valley High would sell hot chocolate. But beneath all that was something deeper — the knowledge that their kids were growing up right in front of them.

They saw it in the way the boys carried themselves. In the way they talked about practice. In the way they treated each other.

The championship wasn't just a game.

It was a milestone.

And it was a test.

As the week stretched on, the excitement built. The Ponies — now spectators — came to every Midget practice, cheering them on, offering tips, acting like older brothers. Some of the Pee Wees watched from the sidelines, eyes wide, imagining themselves under those bright lights someday.

By Friday night, the whole town felt electric.

The Midgets were ready. The coaches were ready. The parents were ready. Galesburg was ready.

The championship game was coming — and the Raiders were walking into it with pride, purpose, and the weight of a town behind them.

Later that evening, after the final practice before the big game, Tom sat on the back porch with his dad. The air was cool, the stars sharp above them, and the hum of the coal breaker in the distance felt like part of the conversation.

Cy didn't start with football.

He never did.

"You and Chris seem close," he said, staring out into the yard.

Tom felt his face warm. "Yeah. We are."

Cy nodded slowly. "You're at that age where things start to matter in a different way."

Tom didn't say anything. He didn't need to.

Cy continued, voice softer than usual. "Girls… relationships… they're not about impressing someone. They're about being honest. Being steady. Showing up when it counts."

Tom swallowed. "I'm trying."

"I know you are." Cy finally looked at him. "And I'm proud of you. Not for touchdowns. Not for wins. For the way you're growing up."

Tom blinked hard, the words hitting deeper than he expected.

Cy leaned back in his chair. "Chris seems like someone who sees you. Really sees you. That's rare. Don't rush it. Don't pretend. Just be the kid you were this season — the one who played with heart and walked her home with respect."

He paused, then added the part he knew mattered most.

"When you step on that field next week, you can't be thinking about impressing her or proving something. That's when players get hurt or make mistakes. You also can't try to be a hero. Heroes don't come from forcing it. They come from doing what's right in the moment, naturally."

Cy put a hand on Tom's shoulder.

"Play your game. Be steady. Be yourself. If you do that, everything else — football, Chris, all of it — will fall into place."

Tom nodded, throat tight. "Thanks, Dad."

BRING IT HOME

The buses rolled into East Valley High just after noon, windshield wipers swiping rhythmically against a steady drizzle. Fog hung low over the stadium, soft and gray, curling around the bleachers and drifting across the turf like smoke. The towering lights were already on, their beams slicing through the haze and casting long, ghostly shadows that made the field look bigger, deeper, and more serious than ever before.

The Midgets stepped off the bus in silence, their cleats clicking on wet pavement, their breath visible in the damp air. The stadium loomed ahead — not loud, not crowded yet, but waiting. The kind of place that demanded respect.

Inside the locker room, the boys found themselves in a space that felt almost sacred. Polished wood benches. Clean white walls. Rows of gleaming lockers. The hum of the lights overhead. It was quiet, but not still — the kind of quiet that comes before something important.

Cy stood in front of them, rain dripping from the brim of his cap, eyes steady. He didn't raise his voice. He didn't pace. He just spoke.

"You've earned this," he said. "Every single one of you. Not because of the record. Not because of the scoreboard. But because of the road that got you here."

He looked around the room — at Eddie Fisher, calm and focused; at Tony Matz, bouncing his knee; at Marcus, nodding slowly; at Tom, sitting tall, eyes locked in.

"We've had ups. We've had downs. We've had moments where we didn't know if this league would even survive. But you showed up. You worked. You believed. And this town — a place with coal in its bones and pride in its people — believed in you right back."

He paused, letting the silence settle.

"Today isn't about being perfect. It's not about being heroes. Heroes don't get made in locker rooms. They show up in moments. And those moments come from heart. From effort. From doing the right thing when it's hard."

Cy stepped forward, voice low but firm. "So when you take that field, don't play for the scoreboard. Play for each other. Play for the coaches who stood beside you. Play for the parents who drove you to practice. Play for the Pee Wee kids watching from the sidelines. Play for the town that never stopped believing."

He looked at Tom. "And play like you know who you are."

No one spoke. No one needed to. They just stood.

And they were ready.

The tunnel smelled like wet turf and adrenaline. As the Midgets jogged toward the entrance, the fog thickened, swirling under the stadium lights like something alive. And then they saw it — the crowd, the largest they had ever played for. People had driven in from every corner of Galesburg, caravanning through the drizzle with headlights glowing in the fog, determined to claim their seats before kickoff.

By the time the boys reached the field, the stands were nearly full — umbrellas clustered together, blankets draped over laps, rally signs propped against the railings. When the Raiders stepped out of the tunnel, their families erupted — waving, cheering, calling their names — a wall of support that made the moment feel bigger than football.

The cheerleaders' banner stretched wide across the gate:

RAIDERS BELIEVE. BRING IT HOME.

Painted in bold blue on white paper, it rippled in the breeze, rain speckling the edges. The boys didn't hesitate. They ran through it together, the banner tearing in a burst of motion and pride.

All around the stadium, rally signs waved in the mist:

GO SWANNY!
RAIDERS NEVER QUIT!
GALESBURG BELIEVES!

Parents stood shoulder to shoulder, bundled in jackets, clapping until their hands stung. The Ponies lined the fence, shouting encouragement. Even some of the Pee Wees had made signs — crooked letters, glitter, duct tape — held high with wide-eyed wonder.

Tom jogged to midfield, helmet in hand, and looked around.

The fog. The lights. The roar of the crowd. And the knowledge that the game would be filmed and aired back home.

It didn't make him nervous.

It made him ready.

He thought about Week Five. He thought about Chris.

He thought about his dad's words:

HEROES COME FROM DOING THE RIGHT THING WHEN IT'S HARD.

This wasn't his moment to be a hero.

It was his moment to be himself.

The Raiders lined up for the opening kickoff, drizzle falling in a thin, steady mist. Fog drifted across the field in slow curls, and the stadium lights glowed like pale suns behind it. The turf squished under their cleats — soft, slick, unpredictable. The kind of field where one slip could change everything.

The whistle blew. The ball sailed into the gray sky.

The championship had begun.

From the first snap, it was clear both teams were evenly matched. The Railers were just as tough as they'd been in Week Five — disciplined, physical, unshaken by the weather. Every run was a battle. Every pass was a risk. Every tackle sent mud flying.

By halftime, the scoreboard still read 0–0. Not for lack of effort — but because neither team would give an inch.

The boys jogged to the locker room soaked, muddy, and breathing hard. But they weren't discouraged. They were locked in.

Cy stepped into the center of the room, hands on his hips, eyes moving from one boy to the next.

"Listen to me," he said, voice steady. "It's 0–0, and that scoreboard doesn't tell the truth about who you are. You've taken their best shot for two quarters, and you're still standing. That's heart. That's toughness. That's everything we've worked for."

He crouched slightly, bringing himself eye-level with them.

"Championships aren't won by perfect teams. They're won by teams that refuse to break. Teams that trust each other. Teams that decide, right now, that they're willing to give just a little more than the guy across from them."

He tapped his chest.

"You've got more in here than you know."

Cy stood tall again.

"So when you walk back out there, don't play scared. Don't play tight. Play like Raiders. Play like a team that knows who it is. Leave everything you've got on that field, and whatever the scoreboard says at the end, you'll know you gave this town, this team, and yourselves something to be proud of."

Midway through the third quarter, the Raiders finally found their moment.

Marcus broke free on a counter play, slipping through a gap Eddie Fisher carved open and churning through the mud for twenty yards. Two plays later, a short out route set them up inside the ten.

On the next snap, Marcus punched it in.

The stands erupted — umbrellas waving, signs shaking in the mist.

Raiders 7, Railers 0.

But the Railers weren't done.

On their next possession, they lined up in the same formation they'd used in Week Five — the one that had fooled Tom, the one that had haunted him for months. The quarterback pitched the ball to the running back, who slowed, cocked his arm, and looked downfield.

The trick play.

The same one.

But Tom didn't bite this time.

He stayed home. He read the eyes. He broke on the ball.

And he caught it.

A clean interception, swallowed by cheers and the pounding of his own heart. His teammates mobbed him, helmets slapping, voices shouting his name.

It wasn't just a play.

It was redemption.

Quiet. Earned. Complete.

The fourth quarter dragged like a fistfight. The field grew worse — patches of mud, puddles forming, footing unpredictable. With just under two minutes left, the Railers mounted one last drive. They pushed, slipped, recovered, and pushed again, inching toward the end zone.

And with 2:12 on the clock, they scored.

The crowd held its breath as their kicker lined up for the extra point. The snap was good. The hold was clean.

But the plant foot wasn't.

He slipped. The ball hooked wide.

7–6.

The fog swallowed the gasp.

The Railers kicked off, pinned the Raiders deep, and forced a quick three-and-out. With a minute left, they had the ball again — and momentum.

The first play was a sweep. The second, a short pass. The third, a misdirection that nearly broke free.

Then came the play that changed everything.

Tony Matz blitzed off the edge, low and fast, his cleats somehow finding traction where no one else's had. He hit the quarterback clean, shoulder to the ball, and the ball popped loose into the mud.

Tony didn't hesitate.

He dove. He covered it. He held on.

The sideline exploded.

The Raiders' offense came out, took a knee, and the clock drained away into the fog.

When the final whistle blew, Tom and Tony found each other in the chaos — muddy, soaked, exhausted, and grinning like kids who had just lived the moment they'd dreamed about.

Friends. Teammates. Heroes — not because they tried to be, but because the moment asked, and they answered.

The Raiders had done it.

Not perfectly. Not easily. But with heart.

Exactly the way Cy said it mattered.

The locker room was a storm of noise — helmets clattering, boys shouting, coaches hugging players, steam rising from soaked jerseys. Mud dripped from cleats onto the tile floor, and the air smelled like sweat, rain, and victory.

But when Cy stepped forward, the room quieted almost instantly.

Joanne stood just behind him, still in her raincoat, hair damp, eyes shining with pride. She had been there for every fundraiser, every equipment order, every late-night planning session, every moment Cy doubted whether the league would survive.

She deserved this as much as anyone.

Cy took a breath, looking at each boy — really looking.

"You did it," he said softly. "Not because you were the biggest. Not because you were the fastest. But because you had heart. Every single one of you."

He gestured toward Joanne.

"And none of this — not this league, not this team, not this moment — would have happened without her. She kept us going when things got tough. She believed in all of you before you even put on a jersey. I want to thank her for everything she's done these past few years — more than most people will ever know."

The boys erupted into applause, stomping cleats and whistling. Joanne blushed, waving them off, but her smile said everything.

Cy continued, voice thick with emotion. "Tonight, you showed what it means to be Raiders. You fought. You trusted each other. You stayed true to who you are. And that's what wins games like this. Not luck. Not tricks. Heart."

He paused.

"You'll remember this day for the rest of your lives. And you earned every second of it."

Outside, the drizzle softened to a mist as families gathered for the ride home. Tom stepped out of the locker room, hair damp, jersey stuffed into his duffel. He spotted Chris waiting near the buses, hands tucked into her sleeves, breath visible in the cool air.

When she saw him, her face lit up.

"You were amazing," she said. "That interception… I mean… wow."

Tom laughed, rubbing the back of his neck. "I just did what I was supposed to do."

"No," she said gently. "You did more than that."

For a moment, they just stood there, fog curling around them, the muffled sounds of celebration behind them. Tom felt something settle inside him — a calm, steady warmth that had nothing to do with football.

"I'm really glad you were here," he said.

"I wouldn't have missed it."

He hesitated. "Now that the season's over… maybe we could hang out more. Not just after games."

Chris smiled, soft and sure. "I'd like that."

It wasn't dramatic. It wasn't loud.

But it was real.

Tom glanced back at the stadium one last time, then toward the bus where his teammates were loading up. He felt taller somehow. Older. Ready for whatever came next.

And as he and Chris walked toward their families, side by side, the night didn't feel cold at all.

The bus rumbled out of the East Valley High parking lot, headlights cutting through the fog as the drizzle finally eased. Inside, the boys buzzed — tired, muddy, bruised, but glowing with the kind of joy that only comes from doing something hard and doing it right.

The championship trophy — small, simple, perfect — sat on the dashboard like it belonged there.

Cy settled into the front seat, finally letting his shoulders relax. Joanne sat beside him, her hand resting lightly on his arm.

"You did good, Cy," she said.

He shook his head. "They did good."

She squeezed his arm. "You helped them believe they could."

Cy looked back at the rows of boys — laughing, replaying plays, nudging each other, still riding the high of the win. Mud streaked their faces. Their hair was plastered to their foreheads. They looked exhausted and alive all at once.

He felt something warm settle in his chest.

Just then, someone — probably Tony — started pounding on the seat with both hands. Another kid joined in. Then another. Soon the whole bus vibrated with rhythm.

And then the chant started.

Low at first. Then louder. Then roaring.

"WE ARE THE RAIDERS…"

"MIGHTY, MIGHTY RAIDERS…"

"ROUGH, TOUGH RAIDERS…"

"ASS-KICKING RAIDERS!"

Cy turned sharply — the kind of look that usually meant *cut it out right now*. The boys froze.

But instead, Cy's mouth twitched.

Then he winked.

And then — to their absolute shock — he joined in.

Louder than all of them.

Joanne laughed as the bus erupted in cheers and the chant thundered through the foggy night.

"WE ARE THE RAIDERS…"

"MIGHTY, MIGHTY RAIDERS…"

"ROUGH, TOUGH RAIDERS…"

"ASS-KICKING RAIDERS!"

The sound rolled out into the dark, echoing off wet pavement, rising above the drizzle, carrying all the pride and heart of a team — and a town — that had earned every bit of this moment.

And that's how the season ended.

Not with speeches. Not with trophies. But with a bus full of boys singing their hearts out, a coach who believed in them, and a town that always would.

EPILOGUE: A STORY REMEMBERED

This story happened forty-seven years ago, during a time when my teammates — my friends and I were caught between being children and becoming men. That final year, just before high school, was a season of guiding moments, bruises, and heart — and the lessons we learned on that field stayed with us in ways we couldn't have understood back then.

Not all of what you've read is strictly true. I had no way of knowing every detail — what every coach said or the exact conversations or ideas that shaped those early days. Time blurs the edges. Memories fade. But the spirit of it all, the feeling of that final glorious season of the Mighty, Mighty Raiders, has stayed with me. So I filled in the gaps the best I could, guided by what I remember, what I felt would provide content without sacrificing merit, and what those moments meant to us.

I wrote this book not just to remember, but to preserve something that feels increasingly rare. In a world shifting from analog to digital, where relationships are often filtered through screens and algorithms, I wanted to capture the simplicity and depth of a time when showing up — really showing up — meant everything.

We were the Raiders. We were teammates. We were kids trying to figure out who we were.

Some of us went on to college. I did, and built a career as an Aerospace Engineer. Others scraped through life, never quite making it out of that town. Still others were taken too soon — names I remember, faces I still see in my mind when I think about that muddy field and the lights cutting through the fog.

I lost touch with many of my teammates over the years. I've heard rumblings, fragments of stories, bits of news. But what I know for sure is that every one of us carried something from that season — a lesson, a moment, a feeling — into the rest of our lives.

I started writing this book twenty years ago, picking it up and putting it down, always assuming there would be plenty of time to finish it. Life has a way of convincing you that tomorrow is guaranteed. Then I was diagnosed with cancer, and everything sharpened. The story that had lived inside me for decades — this story of boys becoming men, of community, of grit and heart — suddenly felt urgent. It wasn't just nostalgia anymore. It was something that needed to be told while I still had the chance, something I wanted to leave behind for anyone who ever wondered what those days meant to us, and what they still mean to me.

This story needed to be told. Not because it's perfect. But because it's real.

And in the end, that's what matters most.

The G.H.A.C. Raiders

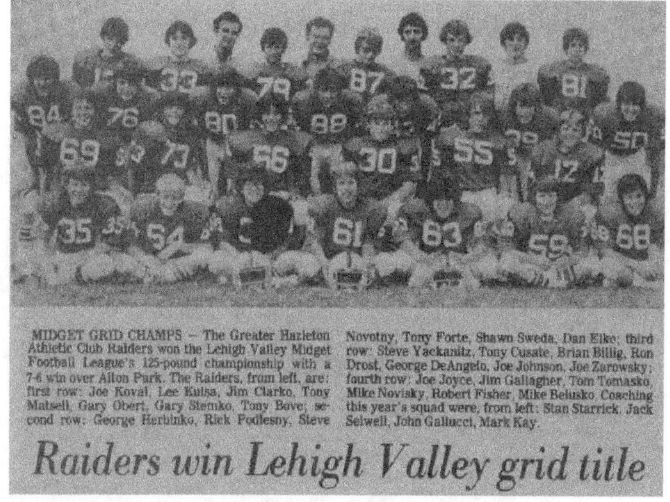

MIDGET GRID CHAMPS — The Greater Hazleton Athletic Club Raiders won the Lehigh Valley Midget Football League's 125-pound championship with a 7-6 win over Alton Park. The Raiders, from left, are: first row: Joe Koval, Lee Kulsa, Jim Clarko, Tony Matsell, Gary Obert, Gary Stemko, Tony Bove; second row: George Herbinko, Rick Podlesny, Steve Novotny, Tony Forte, Shawn Sweda, Dan Elko; third row: Steve Yackanitz, Tony Cusate, Brian Billig, Ron Drost, George DeAngelo, Joe Johnson, Joe Zarowsky; fourth row: Joe Joyce, Jim Gallagher, Tom Tomasko, Mike Novisky, Robert Fisher, Mike Belusko. Coaching this year's squad were, from left: Stan Starrick, Jack Selwell, John Gallucci, Mark Kay.

Raiders win Lehigh Valley grid title

On a late November day in 1979, an article in the Hazleton, Pennsylvania, Standard-Speaker read:

"The Greater Hazleton Athletic Club Raiders captured the championship of the Lehigh Valley Midget Football League's 125-pound class by edging Alton Park by a 7-6 score on a mud-slicked Easton High School field."

"The Raiders concluded their season with a 10-0-1 record and avenged the only blemish on their season with the victory. The Comets had held Hazleton to a 6-6 tie in the fifth game of the season."

Most people didn't realize that the article chronicled an unlikely end to an incredible season — and a fantastic journey. A journey full of obstacles, dotted with episodes of individual inner strength and commitment, as well as solidarity among a group of young men trying to find their way to adulthood. This was my team, and it was this journey that inspired the story told on the pages of this book.